Jaden

Hathaway House, Book 10

Dale Mayer

Books in This Series:

JADEN: HATHAWAY HOUSE, BOOK 10
Dale Mayer
Valley Publishing Ltd.

Copyright © 2020

ISBN-13: 978-1-773363-60-8
Print Edition

About This Book

Welcome to Hathaway House. Rehab Center. Safe Haven. Second chance at life and love.

Jaden Hancock is blessed to still have two arms and two legs, but the one leg is so badly damaged as to be virtually useless. Until he came to Hathaway House, he'd never expected that it might become a vital part of his future. He's willing to work for it, it's just hard to see the lack of progress even after weeks. He knows he needs to accept his current state, but that feels like giving up. And that's something he's not prepared to do. But as defeat, and hope, and depression and final triumph he sees a future he'd never been able to envision before.

Brianna Kole slowly adjusted to Hathaway House. She'd crossed the country to get away from her old life. As the newest staff member, she was polite but not overly friendly. She'd built walls to protect herself from getting hurt again. Only she'd arrived close to the same time as Jaden and in spite of her reservations they'd hit it off instinctively gravitating to the other new guy. But it wasn't long before she was questioning her feelings… and his.

It seems one step forward, then one step backwards. Will these two figure out what's really important? Before it's too late?

Prologue

JADEN HANCOCK STARED at the email from his buddy. He typed in a quick response. **Is this for real, or are you just full of it?** He sent it back just as fast. He watched and waited until he got a reply. Iain had been at Hathaway House for several months now. Jaden had heard a few intermittent responses but nothing major—until this one, where Iain said he was a new man, and life was great. If there was any way Jaden could make it happen, he would be coming to Hathaway House too. But, instead of an email coming in, his phone buzzed. He stared at it in surprise and said, "Iain, is that you?"

"It is," said the boisterous voice of his old friend. "And, no, I'm not full of shit. I've done a tremendous amount of growth and improvement here. Coming to Hathaway House was the best thing I could have done."

"Just because it was good for you doesn't mean I should do it," Jaden said cautiously. "I don't travel well."

"Then don't take a truck, like I did," Iain urged immediately. "You know how I felt about that. It was the worst mistake ever. It put me back weeks."

"Well, I don't have a whole lot of choice," he said. "I'm not sure exactly how I would get there, but just traveling alone would probably kill my back."

"And I also know that you think this is as far as you can

1

go and that you've already adapted and that you've already moved on, so why bother? Right? I'm here to tell you that you can go a whole lot further physically."

"Says you," Jaden scoffed.

"Absolutely, I say so. I've got a call in to Lance too because I think both of you in particular could do well here."

"Maybe. But just the thought of having new medical staff and of starting all over again, explaining the problems, the difficulties, and the pain ..."

"I get it," Iain said. "I really do. I just don't want you to shortchange what could be much improved on a physical level. I'll send you some photos here in a minute. Of course they're not terribly pretty, but they show the progress on my leg. And it exceeds the progress as we were told to expect."

"Sure, but you had surgery. You've had lots of improvements. You're as good as you'll get."

"No, that's the mentality from where you're at," Iain said quietly. "I'm at a much further place."

"So, does that mean you're done with rehab now?"

"No, not quite," he said, "but I can see the end in sight."

"You certainly sound different," Jaden said with a frown. His buddy really did sound good, healthy, happy. He sounded like he was a completely new person. "What brought that about?"

"A lot of things," Iain admitted. "A partner for one. My physical health back for another. My future. All of those things are dead important."

"Did you land a partner?" Jaden sagged in his wheelchair in a daze. "I thought you figured that would never happen?"

"And I figured wrong," Iain said firmly. "Along with my mind-set, I needed to shift a lot. And sometimes, when you're stuck in the same place, you just don't see how different some other place can be."

"It's not so bad here."

"You want to stay there?"

"No," Jaden said, looking around. "It's pretty damn crowded, and it's starting to look like we're all the same."

"So come here," Iain urged. "Try something different."

"How different?" Jaden asked. He stared down at his hands and wondered what happened to the big, stalwart, and strapping young man he'd been, up for any new adventure possible. Ever since he'd been injured, his world had coalesced into this little tiny circle around him.

In a way, it was how he liked it. It was safe. The thought of moving to a new state, moving to a whole new medical team where he'd have to be reinterviewed and reexamined and poked and prodded all over again was enough to make the bile rise up the back of his throat and to give an instinctive and immediate *no* to the plan. But he also knew that Iain had been in a very similar position as Jaden. And, if Iain had had progress, what were the chances of progress for Jaden?

Then he shook his head. No, there wouldn't be any because this was definitely a case of where was no progress available for Jaden. He'd already become as good as he could get. He wouldn't get any better, even if here—or there—a little bit longer.

While he listened, Iain talked about the food and the pool and the people and the animals. Jaden was more than a little shocked. When he finally put down the phone at the end of their conversation, Jaden stared out the window. He was sitting in a large lounge, and about twelve of them were watching a football game on TV. All of their wheelchairs were lined up, like geriatric patients. People had gotten into the same mind-set here, and that's what he understood now that Iain had seen for himself in places like this.

Jaden had become part of the norm, and that norm became his reality, and anything else looked scary and different and impossible to achieve. He wheeled himself back ever-so-slightly, distancing himself a little bit, to see just what was possible.

When his phone buzzed again, he looked down to see images of Iain's leg—the original leg, which he'd certainly seen right after his buddy's surgery. That hamburger blue-black and red gross-looking thing was supposed to be a leg, and then several more photos popped up, showing the improvements. Jaden stared in surprise. Of course his own leg would heal naturally anyway, and it would look a whole lot better with time, even if he stayed here. But when he got to the next picture of Iain's leg, where it showed a strong and fit, heavily muscled leg, followed then by the picture of Iain himself standing on a prosthetic, with no wheelchair or crutches, and a beautiful woman at his side, Jaden's heart lurched.

Damn, he badly wanted something like that for himself. His one good leg was okay. As for his other leg, the doctors had managed to save it, but it was a facsimile of the hamburger that Iain had started with. But just to think that maybe Jaden wouldn't need crutches or a wheelchair down the road? That would be incredible.

He stared at the wheelchair in the first picture of Iain's leg for a long moment. And then, with determination, Jaden headed back to his room. Somewhere online had to be an application or a phone number that he could call and see about getting in that same center. He sent his buddy a text. **Put in a good word for me**, he said. **If there's a space, I**

really want my name on that next available bed.
It's as good as done came back the instant response.
Now, phone them, and then send in your application
with whatever medical documents they need. You
won't regret it. I can promise you that.

Chapter 1

T HE TRIP HAD been brutal, but Jaden was here. At least he would be, as soon as he got checked in and out of this front reception area. People were coming and going, and for some reason he hadn't expected this much movement inside. A huge orderly was behind him and patiently stood to the side as a group wandered outside. Jaden looked around the reception area. Offices were on the left, and great big hallways headed off in two directions, with him sitting at the right-hand corner. A woman stepped out of one of the offices and smiled at him. He looked up and frowned.

"I'm Dani Hathaway," she said, as she reached out a hand.

His eyebrows shot up in surprise. "Hi," he said. "Thank you for accepting me."

She nodded with a big smile. "I have to admit that Iain gave you a great reference."

"Yeah," he said. "He gave you a really big reference too."

"I have your Hathaway House introductory packet here," she said. "Let's get you settled into your room."

She led the way down the hallway, and he followed, only because the orderly behind him was pushing. Jaden wasn't sure he was up for much more than that. The pain in his right shoulder was agonizing, and he was leaning away from it by constantly slouching in the wheelchair. He had been told before how that wasn't a good thing, but it's pretty hard not to favor his right side.

"Let me tell you a little bit about how the process here works," she said.

He listened intently, accepting the Welcome folder and iPad as they walked. He'd heard some about this from Iain, and so Jaden understood a full team would look after him, and everybody would come to see him after he'd procured his room.

When he had told Iain the good news, Iain had spent hours on the phone with him, filling him in on how the system worked. But that wasn't the same thing as actually being here and seeing it for himself. When they got to one of the rooms, she pushed open a door, and he was wheeled inside, noting a large comfortable-looking bed and all the overhead equipment that went with anybody who was physically disabled.

He stared and studied the bars. "One day, I'd rather not have those there."

"When you leave here," she said, still smiling, "it's our hope that we don't have to worry about getting any of this installed in your future home."

He looked at her in surprise and then slowly nodded. He didn't say what was in the back of his mind, which was that he never really expected to return to independent living. He'd been living in the VA system for so long that he forgot another world was out there.

This was a new world.

He wheeled himself slowly to the window, almost floor to ceiling, low enough that he saw out, even in his wheelchair. "Green grass and horses," he murmured. But his eye caught a great big Newfoundlander dog, walking beside a man. And the dog, although it only had three legs, didn't appear to be impeded at all. "And injured animals," he muttered. He shook his head. "You've put together quite a place."

She smiled a warm all-embracing smile that had him settling back and relaxing that much more. "It's been a labor of love," she admitted. "My father was in a similar situation to you and was not getting the help he needed. We decided that we had to do it ourselves then."

"This all came out of helping your father?" he asked in astonishment.

She smiled and nodded. "That's exactly what happened. And, once you start down that pathway, there's no option to get off. It was a merry-go-round for a long time. Now, it's as well-run a business as we can possibly make it."

He placed his tablet on the nearby nightstand, and Jaden realized that the orderly who had brought him in had long gone.

Dani asked, "Is there anything else you could use right now?"

He groaned and said, "Honestly, I'd like to get out of this chair and up on that bed. And I'm not sure when meals are delivered." But then he stopped and frowned. "Or do I have to get my own?"

"Not today, you don't," she said. "And, in fact, not any day, if you're not able."

Just hearing that last word had his back stiffening.

"After a long trip, we don't expect anybody to make it down there on their own. However, if you would like to get a tour, I'd be happy to take you." He hesitated, then there was a bang on the door. And in walked Iain, a great big grin on his face. Dani smiled and said, "Or I'll let Iain take you for a tour."

"That sounds great, thanks very much" Jaden muttered as Dani turned and walked away, but he was in shock. Iain looked robust and healthy. Jaden stared at his buddy and shook his head. "My God, look at you."

"I know," Iain said. "And I look at you, and I see how far I've come because, when I arrived, I was the same as you. So, you take a look at how I am right now and know that this is possible."

Jaden was too dazed to even come back with a joke, but it was almost impossible to envision that much progress in his own body. He slowly shook his head.

Iain said, "Let's go for a ride."

"Okay," Jaden said, "but I can't handle too much."

"A cup of coffee out in the sun? A bite to eat? Ice cream?"

"All of the above," he said with a smile. "I might manage that long."

"If the wheelchair is too uncomfortable," Iain said, "we can get you some pillows too."

At Jaden's headshake, his buddy pushed Jaden down the long hallway that he had seen from the front entrance and now his doorway and then turned a corner, where a large open game room area was. Jaden saw dozens of men in various stages of recovery. This looked more like what he was used to, but Iain kept pushing him forward to a huge dining room cafeteria.

As he took him up to the front, Iain said, "You would probably do well not to eat yet because dinner is in about an hour, but we can do coffee and something right now."

Jaden's stomach grumbled, but he also knew that his stomach was pretty touchy. If he ate too much rich food at one time, he would pay for it.

"Hey, Dennis," Iain said to a huge man on the other side of the cafeteria line.

"Hey. How you doing, Iain. New guy, huh?"

Iain quickly made the introductions. Dennis leaned on the counter and reached over to shake Jaden's hand. "Welcome to Hathaway," he said. "You'll love it here."

Jaden was already finding it different and unique, especially having this level of personableness. He smiled and said, "Apparently dinner is coming up. Is that true?"

Dennis nodded and said, "We'll start serving in about an hour and twenty minutes. If you're hungry right now, let me know. Otherwise we've got coffee and some stuff over here." And he led the way to the coolers, where bottles of juice and milk and water were. When here, he said, "We always have hot coffee, hot tea, and boiled water. You can have soup, noodles, and anything along that line if you want it at any time. Plus, in this display case," he said, "we've always got muffins and cookies and cakes. Something is around at any time. But, if you're hungry for breakfast, lunch, or dinner outside normal mealtime hours, just let me know, and I'll get you something."

Jaden smiled, shook his head, and said, "Coffee right now would be lovely." Then he paused and pointed at Iain. "He did mention ice cream though."

Iain gave a big laugh. "Dennis, you got any ice cream left?"

"What do you guys want? Bars or a cone?"

"A cone would be good," he said.

Dennis grinned and said, "Go on outside with your coffees. I'll bring them." And he disappeared into the back.

And, with the coffee carried by Iain, the two of them

slowly worked their way outside to where more tables were. And then Jaden realized that the whole back wall to the dining room opened up to a deck. "Wow," he said. "So, we can sit outside?"

"That's why the tables are here," he said. "I sit out here quite a bit. But you've got to watch the afternoon sun. It can be brutal." As it was, today was an overcast day. It was still hot, but they found a table partially in the shade. It would take Jaden a bit to adjust to the Texas heat.

"You really are happy you came?" Jaden asked Iain.

"I am, indeed," Iain said. "Now I feel normal again. I don't feel like I'm disabled."

At that, Jaden dropped his gaze to his cup and nodded.

"Hey, I understand," Iain said, leaning forward. "I really do. When I got here, I wasn't in very good shape. I was stubborn, prideful, and I needed to understand that it was up to me."

"Got it," he said. He smiled as he looked around. "And what's this about a girlfriend?"

"She works at the vet's clinic downstairs," Iain said comfortably. "If you're up for meeting her at dinnertime, we can do that. But, if you need to rest, then just say so."

"It depends on how much longer and what else is on my day," he said, while stifling a yawn. "Still seems like a lot of traveling and wreckage to my body."

"It is," Iain said. "And we still have to take things slow and build you back up to your pretrip strength, but you will see people like me here too."

"I have seen a couple," Jaden said. "They don't look like they belong."

"Chances are they are leaving any day," Iain said. "Like me."

Jaden stared at him, his stomach sinking. "You are getting discharged soon?"

"I've got another ten days," he said. "I was really hoping you'd get here before I left."

"What about the girlfriend?"

He grinned. "I'm getting a place in town, which is only a twenty-minute drive away," he said. "I'll set up a center for veterans somewhere here and help them find what they need to do with their life after rehab and get them either training or jobs."

"Aren't there government centers for that?"

"There sure are," Iain said in disgust. "And, to the greater extent, they're useless. I'm hoping that I can end up helping out some of these guys."

"Will you charge for this?" Jaden asked with interest. "Because you know we all get pensions and whatnot, but it's not a whole lot to live on."

"My pension is doing okay," he said. "And I do have other money saved, and it's earning interest. So I'll see what I need initially to set up a free training center. It's the overhead that might kill me. I'll need an office too."

"Right. You have to pay rent and power and water, et cetera."

"So I'm talking with a couple charities in town, plus with a group of men in New Mexico, one of whom I know. Do you know Badger's group?"

Jaden frowned as he thought about it. "You mean Erick's group?"

"Yep. Badger and Erick and about five other guys. They have a similar setup out of New Mexico that they started. Titanium Corp."

At that, his confusion cleared, and Jaden nodded. "I've

heard of Titanium Corp. If you could do something like that here," he said, "wow."

"Well, they're doing a lot of security business and hiring the guys for jobs like that, even some government assignments. Also they have this side gig where they rehab homes, specifically for vets in mind," he said. "That's not what I'm heading into. At least I don't think so." He stopped and stared out the window, frowning as if the ideas were rolling around in his head.

"I think the world is your oyster," Jaden said. "If you can make it happen, then go for it."

"It's just me though," Iain said. "I might need somebody at my side to give me a hand." He studied Jaden thoughtfully.

"Depends how I progress through this place," Jaden said. "But if you're interested in a partner down the road, think about me."

"Will do," Iain said. "First and foremost, you have to look after yourself though. That's the rule here. If it's part of your healing and if it's necessary for your growth, it has to happen. But, if you're doing it for somebody else, Hathaway House wants you to stop right now and to reassess what it is that *you* want in life."

"That's odd to think about," he murmured, remembering how, long ago, his dad took off with his brother to places unknown, leaving him with his mother, who was killed in a car accident soon afterward, forcing Jaden into foster care. "My foster dad passed away about six months ago," he said. "And then my motivation stopped. I didn't know what I was doing any of this for. When you lose your entire family …"

"I get it," Iain said. "The thing is, now it's really clear for you what you're doing and who you're doing it for because there is only you. Maybe that makes it easier. I don't know. Maybe it makes it worse."

"It is what it is," Jaden said in a tired voice. He looked around, realizing that this cafeteria felt more like a restaurant. Not quite like resort dining but maybe a country inn. He nodded toward the fields outside. "It's really nice to see all the green lands."

"Not more apartment buildings and other structures and institutions all around you?" Iain teased.

"Isn't that the truth," he said. "As far as I can tell here, I haven't seen any other people but those associated with Hathaway House."

"Right. Just those tied to the center. Dani has quite a few acres here. I'm not sure how she ended up with it all, but it's not all green, that I can tell you. Just this section around here."

"It's nice to see the horses," Jaden murmured.

"It's even better to ride them," Iain said with a note of satisfaction. "When I got back on a horse again here with Dani at my side, I thought I'd won the lottery," he said.

Jaden looked at him in surprise. "I didn't even know you rode."

"Well, I do," he said. "Like a lot of things in life, we forget because we don't think we can get there again."

"Well, I used to do an awful lot of woodwork," Jaden said. "And I have to admit that I was pretty damn grateful to still have my hands. But this one arm and this one leg ..."

"Yeah, your entire right side took a blow, didn't it?"

"Well, if that's what you call it," he said with a half laugh. "But, yeah, that's the side that took the battering from the accident as we flipped."

"A roadside bomb, right?"

"Yep, sure was," he said. "And, although that shrapnel killed one of my buddies, Tom and I were tossed, burned, and then I ended up half squashed under one of the vehicles. That was the major damage done to the shoulder. The fire pretty well destroyed part of the leg. The shrapnel didn't help either."

"But the other leg is okay?"

"One leg is solid, and one leg is not," he said. "It doesn't make a whole lot of sense, considering how close I was to the bomb and then with the fire raging around us." He shook his head.

Just then Iain's gaze went past his buddy, and his face lit up. "Wait until you see these," he said, a note of satisfaction in his voice.

Jaden twisted ever-so-slightly to see Dennis coming toward them, holding up cones with three scoops of different kinds of ice cream.

He handed them out and said, "You look like guys with appetites."

"Well, I did," Jaden said, "but I'm worn out from the long day of traveling …"

"Make sure you get some muscle relaxants for the night," Dennis warned. "I've seen so many guys arrive and think that a good night's sleep after their transfer here will put them back on the path, only to have a terrible night."

Jaden accepted his ice cream with a big smile and said thank-you sincerely to Dennis.

Dennis nodded and said, "Be back here for food in an hour. You have a two-hour window though. So if you need that nap first, you take it." And he disappeared.

"Coming back to the problem of your accident," Iain said suddenly, "how much of it is in your head?"

Startled, Jaden looked at his buddy and raised his eyebrows. "No more than anybody else's accident is in their head," he said.

"Good," Iain said. "It should make it easier for you to heal."

"Says you," he said. "I've had no improvement or very little improvement in the last many months."

"That's because you gave up," Iain announced.

Bristling at his words, Jaden glared at him.

Iain grinned. "I know you don't want to hear that," he said, "but sometimes you need to hear the truth."

"You mean, the truth that you see," Jaden warned, "because that's not the truth from where I sit."

"Of course not," he said, "because you don't want to see that you could have done more. And, in this case, maybe there *wasn't* more you could have done." Iain gave him a shrug. "I honestly didn't think any further improvement awaited me back at my old place either."

"So you really think this place is what made the difference for you?"

"Absolutely," he said. "Mentally and physically."

"But then there's also your girlfriend," Jaden teased.

"Yes, and no," he said, "but I realized that I had a lot of work to do on myself that only I could work on. I mean, she's come a long way too."

"She has some health issues?"

"No, not really," he said, "but we've all got issues of one kind or another. By the way, you'll need to take a look at your team and make sure you understand who's who and keep your meetings with them. They're here for you."

"I get that," Jaden said. "It's just the thought of going through it all over again, all my injuries, all about my accident, everything that's been done since then …"

"And yet that's probably as vital as anything," Iain said. "Just think about all those new eyes, new brains, and new thought processes now focused on your file. Who knows what they could come up with?"

"Hey, Dennis, do you have another one of those?"

At the light musical voice, Jaden turned slightly to see Dennis standing in front of the counter and a woman nodding at the ice cream cones in his and his buddy's hands. She was a blonde, her hair in a plait down the center of her back. She had that nurse look to her. He smiled and said to Iain, "I guess a lot of beautiful women are here, aren't they?"

"Tons," Iain said. "This one is newer though."

The two of them at the cafeteria line were busy talking, and then Dennis disappeared. She waited at the coffee machine just far enough away that they couldn't say anything to her. When Dennis returned a moment later, he had a single scoop of ice cream in a cone for her. She held it up in a salute to the men, then turned and disappeared.

"Damn," Jaden said. "Maybe I'll like this place for other reasons after all."

At that, Iain's laughter boomed out loud. "I hope so, buddy. I hope so."

BRIANNA KOLE HAD only been on the job not quite four weeks to date and was still figuring out just what was the right way to work and the right wrong way to work. As far as the system went here, it was efficient. But she appreciated a lot of things, like the house rules and the ice cream for one. She wasn't even sure if she was allowed it, but, when she'd seen the two men partaking, she couldn't resist asking Dennis.

Now, she carried her ice cream back to her desk, where she would get out some of that paperwork. She had a lot of files to catch up on. In addition to being a nurse on call to fill in as needed, she also played a part-time IT role here just because it was one of her passions, and definitely some computer issues needed to be looked at here. Dani had some guy in town who came out on a regular basis, but, when some of the other nurses struggled with one of the programs, Brianna would take a look at it. Not that she had any IT background. She was just good with computers.

She stepped into her office, sat down at her desk, looked at the stack of files beside her, and groaned. But that's part of the job, both for her and for medical institutions in general. Keeping meticulous records was important, and, although Hathaway House did an awful lot in digital format, they also maintained paper copies as well. She wasn't exactly sure why, and Dani was looking at potentially changing up the system, but, at the moment, this duality of records was considered the *best practice* in a medical center like this. So, that's what Brianna was doing. She had her work cut out for her.

As she dug in to the next file, she worked away on her ice cream cone too.

Shane, one of the PT guys, stopped in and took one look at her. His eyebrows popped up. "When did we get ice cream?"

"No clue," she said cheerfully, "but I saw two guys in the cafeteria with cones."

"That figures," he said. "Once one guy finds out about it …"

She nodded sagely. "Don't tell me that you won't ask

him for one too."

"Did Dennis give that to you?"

"Yep, he did," she said. "First rule of a new job is to find the people with power and make friends."

Shane burst out laughing and took off.

She grinned in his wake. He was one of the friendliest guys she'd met so far. Not that anybody was unfriendly, but people were fairly serious when dealing with their own issues and also their assigned patients. And she understood. She was a day nurse and supposedly just on a relief basis. Yet that relief basis had turned into so much more. So far, she didn't see a break in her schedule over the next month. While technically part-time, on paper anyway, she now worked full-time hours.

She'd hadn't been here very long, but had already found that she was much needed. In the mornings, she dispensed some of the medications and did some of the rounds. In the afternoons, she did paperwork. She only had an hour left in her shift though, and then it was dinnertime.

Just a few days ago Dani had mentioned that an apartment was available on-site, and Brianna hadn't accepted because she thought to only be here part-time. However, if she were to go full-time, she would definitely reconsider that. She was temporarily staying with a friend in town, but that wasn't something she particularly wanted to do permanently. Plus, if she could avoid commuting—the gas, the wear and tear on her vehicle, not to mention her time involved—that would count up week by week and would save her some money.

Frowning, she checked her watch and realized that maybe she could catch Dani before she left for the afternoon. Brianna raced toward the front offices to see Shane with an ice cream cone in hand. He stood at the edge of Dani's door. He looked at Brianna, grinned, and said, "She's to blame."

She poked her head around to see Dani sitting there, staring at the ice creams the two held. Brianna quickly finished off her cone.

"Once word gets out, Dennis will have a mutiny on his hands," Dani muttered.

Shane took off, and Brianna stepped into Dani's office. "Have you got a moment?"

"Sure," Dani said. "That's about all I have, but, if you can make it fast, then a moment will do."

"Great," Brianna said. She sat down and continued, "You offered me an on-site apartment earlier, and, at the time, I was thinking I would only be here a few days a week. However, it's become full-time since day one almost."

"I was going to ask you about your schedule," Dani said. "One of our nurses just handed in her notice. She was due to have medical surgery herself, but it supposedly wouldn't be for another six months. Now they've moved up her date to next week."

"Oh," Brianna said. "So …" And then she let her voice trail off.

"Could you do full-time now? Come on as permanent staff?"

"What about this nurse, when she's recovered from her surgery?"

"She has asked me not to pin her down as to coming back, but she's a good nurse. So, if she wants to return, when she's back on her feet again, then that's a different story. But her recovery time will be a good six months."

Brianna nodded slowly. "I'm sorry for her."

"I am too, but at least she's getting the surgery now," she

said. "She's also going to spend some of the rehab time in California. Once there, she may not want to return to Texas."

"So, full-time for me? Starting when?" She would love that. One permanent full-time job was what she'd been looking forward to for months.

"Yes," Dani said. "At least as of next Friday, which is her last day."

"You know my schedule is already pretty booked, right? That I'm full-time anyway, as far as the current shifts are set up?"

"And I'll have to take a look at that," Dani said, muttering as she pulled out a batch of hard-copy schedules to place in front of her. "You have another five days booked the week after that."

"Yes," she said. "My scheduled is booked full for the next month."

Dani nodded and shuffled deeper into her pile of employee schedules, eyeing a couple more weeks. She nodded again. They discussed times and shifts to adjust, and then Dani sat back and said, "So, once I get this okayed by the other nurses as I divvy up the workload per shift, I'll run a draft copy of your schedule by you and the others before I finalize anything. That way hopefully we can head off any problems before we end up short on nurses one day or even with too many on another." Dani smirked. "I guess *too many* is never a problem, right?"

Brianna laughed. "Nope. As long as we get our hours, I'm sure everybody's happy."

"So does that mean you also want the apartment now?" Dani asked, focused on Brianna.

"Do you still have it?"

"Yes, plus another nurse is leaving. Her room will be available soon as well."

"Perfect," Brianna said. "I would love to move in here, since that would make my life a lot easier and save me some traveling time and expenses."

"Which is why we have it," Dani said. "We're certainly close enough to town for people to travel there, if they want to, but it's also nice to know that you don't have to."

"Are our meals included?"

"They are, indeed," she said. "Sorry. I should have made sure you knew about that from your first day here. Same deal as always here. Even if you're part-time, you can have your meals here. But, once you're living here, then that's where your meals are expected to be had. Dennis figures that into his food budget. Not that you can't go out to eat elsewhere, but we've got you covered, is all I'm saying. Either way, Dennis likes to have leftovers for those days when we have investors coming, and I've forgotten to tell him."

Dani laughed. "I try not to do that to him too many times during any given month. Oh, as an aside, we do have some apartments with little kitchen units, if you're interested, but this one in particular doesn't have cooking facilities."

"And that suits me," Brianna said. "I've never really had much inclination to cook."

"I love cooking," Dani said, "but I never really have much time for it."

"Life is a little busy in your corner," Brianna said, as she stood. "But speaking of food, you should get one of those ice cream cones before you head home."

"What flavors are there?"

"Well, Dennis gave me maple walnut," she said, "but I know the guys had three different flavors."

She rolled her eyes. "Of course they did. If it wasn't for the medical staff salaries," she said, "I think our food bill would be the next biggest expense here. But it's all good because we are blessed to have our staff and our meals." At that, Dani stood and said, "Let me show you the apartment."

They walked outside past the pool to a long row of apartments. "This side," she said, "has full-size one-bedroom apartments down halfway, and the other half are more like studios. These apartments on the other side are larger, with more bedrooms, for the married staff and their families."

"Right," she said. "That's pretty amazing."

"We don't often have that side full," Dani said, "because a lot of the doctors and nurses live in town and just come back and forth." She led the way to one of the smaller apartments, then opened it up and stepped inside. "This one's still vacant."

Immediately Brianna smiled at the wash of cool air. "This is lovely," she said. "And I don't even need furniture."

"I was going to ask if you need a furnished unit or not," Dani said. "We have both."

"I don't have any, so this is lovely," she said. They walked through to the single bedroom, which was more of a studio setup and then out back to a small private patio. "I love this," she repeated, gasping in surprise at the green rolling hills around her. "It's such a nice place to destress."

"Same rules apply when living on the property as when you're working," Dani said, "but the pool is accessible for you afterhours. Though we do close it down at eleven and the hot tub as well. Patients come first, from seven to five, but after that, the staff members are free to take advantage."

"Thank you so very much, Dani."

Dani reached out, and Brianna realized that keys were in

her hand. She accepted them and said, "I guess I'll head back to town and move in tonight." She couldn't help but laugh in joy too.

Dani smiled and said, "You do that. I'll get the paperwork drawn up for the contract on the property."

"And for my full-time job?"

"And for your full-time job," Dani said with a smile.

As Dani took off, Brianna quickly looked around and grinned. "This is so beautiful," she whispered to herself. She headed back outside. Her workday was done, but she'd left her purse upstairs. She quickly retraced her steps to her office, grabbed her purse and her keys, and headed out to the parking lot. She could have had dinner now too, but, since she had a two-hour window for her meal, she could do that later.

Right now she wanted to get to her friend's house and grab her stuff and then move in here. On the way, she called her friend and quickly told her about the change in plans.

"I'll miss you, but that's perfect," Rosie said. "That sounds like a great idea for you."

"Well, I really appreciate you giving me your couch for so long," she said, "but this is a lovely solution."

"It is, indeed. Will you be in town for dinner?"

"Don't you have your regular book club meeting tonight?"

"I do," she said, "but if you'll be leaving …"

"I'm not really leaving though," she said. "I'll just be a little bit farther away."

"If it's not that big a deal, then we'll maybe set up dinner next week sometime."

"That would be wonderful," she said with a grin. "If you're okay with me coming over now, I'll head straight home to grab my gear and then come back."

"I would love to do something like that too," Rosie said enviously. "It's got to be nicer than my place."

"Your place is great," she said. "But, if I can start my life anew, you know that'll be a good thing too."

"Starting life anew is a *very* good idea," she said. "And a long time coming. Gerald, that nasty ex of yours, left you at the altar and forced your world into a crumbling heap as it was, so I'm really rooting for you on this one."

"Thanks," Brianna said. She hated the mention of her ex since that was still a raw and open wound in many ways. "At least by leaving me at the altar," she said, "I found out about him and my maid of honor having an affair before we were actually married. Not that hearing about someone cheating on you is good at any time." After a moment, she added, "I wonder if they ever got married."

"Your ex and your maid of honor?"

"Yeah. Did you ever hear?"

"I did hear about Gerald and Jenna occasionally afterward. I just didn't tell you," Rosie said. "I didn't want to mention their names and upset you."

"Well, there's upset and then not being upset," Brianna said. "It was pretty rough initially at the time, but whatever."

"They broke up anyway," Rosie said.

Brianna hated the fact that a note of satisfaction settled in her stomach when she heard that. "I should be a bigger person and say, *Oh, I'm really sorry,*" she noted, "but it's really hard for me to find that sympathy. At least not yet."

"No sympathy needed," Rosie said. "Once a louse, always a louse."

Chapter 2

W HEN BRIANNA WAS fully packed up, she made her way back to Hathaway House, loving that she could live here too. She pulled off to the side of the road before she neared the long driveway, so she could overlook the entire ranch ahead of her. She didn't even know what you would call this place, all of it included, but Dani had acres where her horses—and the llama—were, and then she had multiple outbuildings as well as the center itself, which included a veterinarian clinic in the bottom floor.

Brianna had not yet even made her way to see the animals. She had heard about the vet clinic below the main floor where she worked, and she had caught glimpses of the therapy animals being shared with the human patients. Brianna had every intention to check out the animal patients in the clinic as well as the permanent animal residents here. She smiled at that thought and reminded herself to do that. Soon.

She drove carefully toward where the apartments were, then took her assigned parking spot and started unloading everything. She was more than delighted to live here. As she took out her last load, she looked up to see one of the men on the deck above, outside the cafeteria area. She waved a hand and called out, "Good evening."

"Good evening," he said back.

She quickly dropped off that last box to her new apartment and then made her way closer to him, standing on the grass below the upper deck. "Did I miss dinner?"

"I don't think so," he said. "But I just arrived today, so I'm not sure."

She raced up the stairs and recognized him as one of the men who had had the ice cream earlier. She smiled at him. "If you're up for some company," she said, "I'll see if I can grab some food first before my time runs out and then join you."

His eyebrows popped up, and he nodded. "Absolutely," he said. "I'm just finishing."

"Good. Can I get you anything while I'm there?" She turned to look at him as she walked slightly backward to the cafeteria line.

"I might come and get seconds in a bit," he said. "Go ahead and get yours first."

She raced up to see Dennis standing there, cleaning up a lot of the trays. "Did I miss out?"

"Some of it's gone, but we always have something to offer," he said. "What would you like?"

"Just give me a plate of goodness," she said.

He nodded and served her a massive amount of a beautifully unique salad. It had chickpeas and olives, and it looked like a variation of a Greek salad with skewers of meat and some beautiful rice, yellow in color, with vegetables and maybe raisins too, but she didn't quite know for sure. With that cursory glance, she put it on her tray, grabbed a bottle of water and some cutlery, and headed to where the guy was who she'd talked to earlier.

As she placed her tray down, she said, "Thanks for offering to share your table."

"I think here," he said, "we all share."

She smiled, nodded, and said, "I'm Brianna, by the way."

"Jaden," he offered. "And I literally just arrived today, so I don't know anything about the place."

"And I arrived almost four weeks ago," she said with a conspiratorial look. "So we're both newbies."

"Wow," he said. "Yet you act like you're very comfortable here."

"I am to a certain extent," she said. "But now I just moved into one of the resident apartments, and that's made my life a little easier."

"I'm sure it went well then," he said. "You work here?"

"Oh, sorry," she said, as she paused and looked at him. She gave a shake of her head. "Yes, I'm one of the nurses. I was part-time, but now I'm full-time."

"Good for you," he said. "Well, obviously I'm one of the patients."

She smiled and nodded. They ate in companionable silence, and then suddenly Dennis was at her side. "Jaden, how are you doing?"

Jaden looked up at him and smiled. "I think I'm good," he said.

"Do you want any more dessert or other food?"

"I think I'm full. That traveling is likely to upset my system as it is."

"Got it," he said. Dennis took away his plate as well as the rest of his cutlery. "Do you want anything else to drink now?"

Jaden shook his head. "I'll probably crash after this."

"Good enough," he said. He looked over at Brianna. "How are you doing?"

"I'm doing great," she mumbled around a chunk of meat that she'd popped off from the skewer and into her mouth.

Dennis grinned and took off.

"Is everybody this friendly?" Jaden asked. "I came from an institution where people speak in whispers, low voices, and everyone doesn't want to disturb anybody."

"It's not like that here at all," she said.

Just then came several barks.

Jaden turned in surprise to see an older man and a great big Newfoundlander walking toward the edge of the deck. The dog stopped beside Jaden and *woof*ed. Jaden reached out a hand, and the dog immediately came closer, looking for ear scratches.

The older man looked at him, smiled, and said, "I'm the Major," he said. "Dani is my daughter."

Jaden smiled, reached out a hand, and shook it, whereas Brianna stared at him.

"Wow," Brianna said. "You're the one she started this for."

"Yep, in a way," he said. "Although I'd say both of us started this."

Brianna immediately felt embarrassed. "I just heard rumors," she rushed in to save her mistake.

He lifted a hand. "Don't worry about it," he said. "What we've built, we've built. But she has carried it on." He reached down, scratching the dog on her head. "This is Helga. She's around all the time too."

Both of them stopped for a moment to give her a cuddle, but Helga now stared and sniffed at the meat on Brianna's plate.

"Just remember to never feed any of the animals around here," the Major said. "Most of them have stomach issues over the more obvious physical ones, and too much human food just causes them more trouble."

"I've heard about that," Brianna said, giggling, "but Helga is not listening to you."

The Major gave a shout of laughter. "No, she's not, but I'll take her for a walk along the paddocks to distract her and to get her away from this temptation." And he called Helga to his side, and the two descended the stairs and took off toward the fenced-in area. Several of the horses came wandering over to see the Major. He talked with a few of them and then kept going toward the others.

"It's beautiful here," she said dreamily.

"It is," he said. "For you, it's home and work. For me, it's a place to rest and to heal and then to move on."

"A small distinction," she said, "but one that is very important."

"Exactly," he said with half a smile. "And, if you don't mind, I think I'll head to my room now." And he slowly pushed his wheelchair back from the table, pivoted, and headed inside to the cafeteria and beyond.

"Have a good night," she called out. He lifted a hand and wheeled away. She picked up the next piece of souvlaki and dug in. She understood that, for him, this wasn't necessarily an easy place to be. But, for her, well, it was darn near perfection.

JADEN HEADED TO his room. It was barely early evening yet, but he also had several of his medical team members who he expected to stop in to see him, to greet him, to give him tips and pointers and other info. He didn't even know who they all were still. Back in his room, he made his way onto the bed before collapsing in relief. As he did so, a head poked around the corner. He looked up and smiled to see one of his doctors, given the white lab coat.

"I'm Dr. Blackwell," he said. "I hear you've just arrived, and you've been assigned to my team."

"Or you've been assigned to my team," Jaden said with a laugh.

"True enough," the doctor said with a smile. He sat down for a moment in the only chair in the room, and they went over a few of the things that he needed to check up on from Jaden's latest test results. "Your physical file still is not here, but I've been given a short overview, which I've just confirmed here with you," he said. "But, as soon as I get the full medical record on you, I'll review it. For now, do you need anything to help you sleep for the night?"

"Dennis mentioned that I should get some muscle relaxants for my first night," Jaden said, as he stretched out fully now, dropping his head back on the pillow. "But honestly, after all that traveling, I'm pretty tired. So I doubt I'll need any help."

Dr. Blackwell chuckled. "I happen to agree with our armchair advisor, Dennis. I'll leave you a couple muscle relaxants on your bedside table with a glass of water for tonight. That way, you don't have to get up, if you suddenly awake in pain."

Jaden nodded his thanks.

"But feel free to press the Call button at any time, especially for those painful episodes."

"Thanks."

"So are you eating? Are your bowels moving? How is your stress level, from a range of one to ten?"

By the time they were done discussing these matters, and the doctor had gone, Jaden felt even more tired. Two more people poked their heads in. One was Shane for his physical therapy needs, and one was the psychologist, his shrink. Her name, he had already lost track of.

"And don't forget," she said. "A lot of information about a lot of our systems are coming at you real fast and all at once on this your very first day. Don't worry. Everything is on your tablet. You can find and contact any of us anytime you want. Feel free to ask questions of anybody, and, if we don't have the answer, we'll find someone who does."

"Thank you," he said.

As she walked toward the door, she stopped, looked at him, and said, "How do you feel about your recovery so far? From your last rehab center?"

He stared at her blankly.

She raised an eyebrow. "Do you feel like you're *there* yet? Do you feel like you're 100 percent there or 50 percent there or have you just started on this rehab journey?"

"I would have said, prior to coming here, that I was already done," he said. "But I see from Iain that, in his case, a lot more progress was available to be gained."

"*In his case?*"

Jaden nodded. "Because I didn't think something like that was available for me, I thought I'd hit as far as I would go."

"So, let me ask you this," she said, as she walked back into his room a few steps. "Do you feel like you've given up?"

"No," he said, "but I do feel like the medical practice gave up on me."

She smiled a brilliant smile that lit up the room.

"Good," she said.

"That makes you happy? I don't understand." Puzzled he studied her, not sure where she was coming from.

"And we'll talk about that too," she said, "as time goes on. But that's an answer I do love to hear."

"Why is that?"

"Because what it means to me is that you didn't give up on you."

Chapter 3

S EVERAL DAYS LATER Brianna crossed Jaden's path again. She found herself in line behind him at lunch. He was looking decent and chipper but not any different. "Hey," she said. "How are you doing?"

He looked at her in surprise, then recognized her and smiled. "Well, I'm a few days ahead from when we first met," he said.

"Have you adjusted?"

"No," he said with a head shake. "Not sure how long it takes to adjust to the craziness of here. It's so different from the VA hospital. But different in a good way. It's a lot to take in."

She laughed. "Good point," she said with a smile. "I'm a little further along, so I can say that the adjustment gets easier."

"Maybe," he said. "So, far it's tests and meeting people and talking, but ..."

Such disgust was in his tone that she burst out laughing. "You don't want them to jump into something like your rehab when they don't have a plan in place first, do you?"

"No, but I hate waiting," he admitted grudgingly.

At that, Dennis turned to look at him. "So, if you don't like waiting," he said, "what is it you'll have today, young master?"

"You're not that much older than I am," Jaden protested. But they quickly wrangled their way to his food choices.

By the time Jaden had a full plate, she'd sorted out what she wanted. Dennis gave her a plateful of her own, and she headed over to grab water.

"Would you mind getting me one too, please?" Jaden asked, as he held out cutlery for her.

Since they were together and ready at the same time, she asked, "Shall we find a place to sit together?"

"That works for me," he said.

She found a table out in the sun. "It might be too hot," she said, "but it doesn't look we have a whole lot of choices right now."

"No, I think lunch becomes one of the big events, where everybody jumps to attention to be here," he said.

"With good reason," she said. "The food is fantastic."

"I know, right? Best food ever."

Once seated, they quickly tucked into their lunches. By the time he was done, she was almost finished at the same time. She sat back and said, "I really don't want to go back to work today."

"No, me neither," he said. "I still have to meet my nurse too. Well, I met one but not the second one."

"You haven't met her yet?" She frowned, pulled out her iPad from one of the pockets on her scrubs, and looked at her own schedule. "You know what? That could be because you're my patient," she said, frowning and flicking through the pages on her tablet. "I'm sorry. I'm a little behind, playing catch-up. Dani had to do a big shuffle on the schedules because one of the nurses is leaving a lot sooner than expected, and then I was supposed to be just part-time but was full-time ..."

She looked up at him and laughed. "*Anyway,* so then things got really complicated when I was supposed to take on the departing nurse's assignments too." She laughed again, stopped, looked at today's schedule on her tablet, and said, "Jaden Hancock?"

"That's me."

She chuckled. "Well, maybe we can just have coffee and meet each other here right now."

"Or technically we could say that we've *already* met each other," he said with a grin.

She nodded. "I do have to go over your medications though," she said, bringing up his file, newly added to the digital database by Brianna herself. But, by the time they were done with this overview, they were both more comfortable than she'd expected to be. "And I think you're meeting Shane for some testing this afternoon, aren't you?"

"Yeah," he said glumly. "Iain warned me about him."

"Warned you in what way?"

"Shane's really subtle. Nothing happens, nothing happens, and then *bam.* All of a sudden you're in major pain."

"Don't ever let him push you into that stage," she said. "You can tell him to back off."

"I could," he said with a half smile. "But also, if I plan to get out of here in the same shape that Iain is in, I don't want to buck the system too much. If the PTs here know what they're doing, I have to put my trust in them and do it."

"That's a really good way to look at it," she said in approval. "You haven't given up, and that's great. You're here now, so be patient and see what everyone on your team can offer you."

"That was the thought," he said, as he nodded. "And speaking of which ..." He looked up to see Shane walking toward them.

Shane stopped at their table and asked, "Are you guys done eating?"

"Yeah. Why?" Brianna asked him.

"I was hoping Jaden could shift his schedule a bit, so I could work with him earlier," he said. "That way I can run into town to pick up some of the equipment that I missed on its regularly scheduled delivery, and I really need it."

"Sure enough," Jaden said. "I'm ready when you are."

Shane grinned at him. "I hope so," he said. "I've heard that phrase a time or two, but sometimes the men go back to their room in tears."

"Well, let's hope there aren't any tears in my world," Jaden said. "Up until now, I feel like I've already poured every bucketful that was available."

"And you shouldn't be sending them back in tears," Brianna protested. "What about keeping within their limits?"

Shane looked at her in surprise, then saw the frown exchanged between Brianna and Jaden. Shane smiled gently. "We only do as much as he can handle," he said.

Jaden looked at her with a smirk on his face. "Thanks for being worried," he said, winking at her, "but we'll be good." Then he turned and headed after Shane.

She knew most of these patients were military types. She could almost be embarrassed that she was sticking up for this ex-Navy SEAL, afraid the PT guy would hurt Jaden. *Almost.* But her innate caregiver instincts had automatically kicked in. She was all about dealing with their pain in ways to lessen their agony. Plus maybe that maternal instinct in her, awaiting her own babies to care for, was yearning for trial runs with all her patients.

She watched them go, wondering if Jaden would be

okay. But Shane had been here a long time, and she'd never heard anything but good reports about him. However, it really bothered her to think of these men at the end of a day resorting to tears. But then she realized it wasn't a case of resorting to tears of sorrow or even of pain, but maybe tears being released due to the stress of the day, whether physical or mental.

Often women placed unfair expectations on men—any males, whether military or not—to keep their diligence and their silence, and these women expected the men to control their attitudes, even when inside they're breaking. In Brianna's opinion, it was best to avoid pushing them into greater areas of pain and was much better that these patients be allowed to release their pent-up emotions instead, to let go of some of that stress and the weight of responsibility on their shoulders, so that they could turn around and face a new day again. And again and again.

SHANE LED JADEN to one of the rooms he had yet to be in. He wheeled into the center of the room, spun around, and said, "Wow, this is a huge room."

"It is, indeed." Shane tossed a file and a clipboard onto the small table off to the side and laid down his tablet. "So, we've started with some elementary testing," he said, "but the focus appears to be that poor leg of yours and your structural alignment, which is definitely off. Then there is your shoulder."

At that, Jaden's eyebrows rose. "Is it the shoulder too?"

"Definitely, it is. You're blessed in that you still have both legs. But obviously you've been compensating for the poor one," Shane said, as he walked toward him. "The bottom line is, you're also throwing your right shoulder and your spine into that misalignment—your head too. So headaches, difficulty sleeping, and all of those related aches and pains are the result of that."

"What about my gut sensitivities? I had a few issues before the accident, but it's much worse now."

"It depends how many issues you got from the accident itself," Shane said, "but any structural alignment that we can fix now will help you in that regard."

"I like the idea of that," Jaden muttered. "So, where do we start?"

"Well, you won't want to hear this," he said, "but we start with more testing."

Jaden groaned. "I was hoping that we'd start with a workout program."

"You'd be surprised at just how much testing there is before we can get started. I do have a plan set out," he said. "But, first off, we'll take a bunch of photos, so you can see what I'm talking about. I want you to stand up and to step against that wall, so you're as flat against it as you can be."

Jaden nodded, rolled over slowly in his wheelchair, stood up on his good leg, and held his weight off his bad leg as he leaned against the wall.

"Okay, here's a set of crutches," Shane said, holding them up to him. "Use the crutches to help align yourself as straight as you can, with your heels against the wall." With that done, Shane took away the crutches and took several photographs of Jaden from the front, both sides, and then more along his back—just so Jaden could see what Shane saw.

Jaden wore only a muscle shirt and shorts, and he could

feel his bad leg already shrinking with the pain. "Can I get off the leg now?" he asked.

Shane stopped, looked at him, stared down at the leg, and asked, "Which one?"

"The bad one."

And Shane nodded. "Put your weight on the good one and tell me, on a scale of one to ten, how that good leg is holding up."

"It's fine," he said, avoiding the number issue.

"But what's *fine*?" Shane asked quietly. "You've become so accustomed to it taking the weight of everything. Did you ever stop to listen to what its complaints are?"

"Of course not," he said. "It'll just have to suffer in silence because it needs to do its job."

"Agreed," Shane said with a half smile. "But what we need to do is have it do its job without hurting itself any further."

"*Any further?*" Jaden's voice rose at the end. The last thing he wanted to think of was an injury to that leg, his good one.

"Well, it didn't get off scot-free, did it? Didn't you notice the angle that you're holding your good leg at? The angle that you put all your weight on is not quite right," he said. He bent down, then took a photo of just the good leg and stood to hold it up on his camera for Jaden to see. "You can see the angle that you're standing at naturally right now isn't good for the left leg."

"Well, I can shift that," he said.

"Good," Shane said. He handed him the crutches back again. "Now, just like I asked you to earlier, position yourself naturally on both your legs, as straight as you can against that wall, keeping in mind to adjust the angle your left leg has been at currently."

Jaden did as he requested, only to stare down to realize that the left leg did not want to move into a fully straight-forward alignment. He looked up at Shane, his eyebrows raised.

Shane nodded. "See what I mean?"

"I guess," he said, frowning. "I didn't realize that it was struggling so much."

"Well, you've asked it to take on a heavy load," Shane said. "So one of the biggest issues right now is to make sure that whatever load it does carry is something that it can carry long-term. Not just a short-term fix but beyond that." He took more photos of Jaden's alignment and posture so he had documentation as to what Jaden was like when relaxed. Initially. Post-PT.

Shane took several photos when Jaden thought he was straight, when he thought he was leaning from side to side, and then saw the truth in the actual photos. He shook his head in amazement. "And here I thought I was sitting straight up," he said after one particular session. "But, according to those photos, I'm leaning forward."

"And you're leaning forward because of pain in your back," he said. "It's a common issue, but it's one that we need to address fast."

Jaden nodded slowly. "Well, I didn't realize that was even an issue. So, yes, absolutely. It needs to be addressed."

"So, a few other issues need to be dealt with," Shane said. "Let's finish off all this testing, so you have a good idea."

By the time they were done, Jaden was surprisingly tired. "We didn't do anything," he muttered. "And yet I'm already sore."

"Because you're using muscles that don't want to be used in the way that you need them to be used from here on out," Shane explained. "When you allow your posture to slide like that, correcting that will take time because of muscle memory. You've taught them to be this way for the last several months. Now here we need to retrain them. In the meantime, they'll rebel."

"Great," he said. "So now what?"

"Now we'll work on a bit of a massage, although it's not the nice pleasant spa-type massage you're probably thinking of," he said with a chuckle.

"Meaning, it'll hurt, right?"

"Maybe not," he said. "But we'll do some deep breathing exercises to hopefully relax you a bit, and then we'll start working on the intercostal muscles."

Jaden didn't even know which ones those were, but, if Shane said they needed work at this point in time, Jaden was willing to give his PT guy the benefit of the doubt. Jaden had to wonder why none of these issues had come up in his past physiotherapist sessions at the other center. "Is this work common among your profession?"

"Everybody looks at posture slightly differently," he said. "There's a right way and a wrong way in terms of defining *posture*, but, after so many injuries have occurred, especially all concentrated in one spot, a lot of times the posture rehab is relaxed. The medical staff knows that, for some muscles, they can no longer possibly do the same work that they used to do. The trouble is, you still have to get the muscles there to do its maximum job as best as they can."

"Got it," he said, as he wheeled his way slowly to the door. "Where's the massage at?"

"I figured your bed."

"Perfect," he said. "I didn't think I could do much more than get into bed anyway after this."

"I'll be there in about ten minutes," he said. "So, boxers on and the rest off. Stretched out on your stomach with just a sheet on top would be good."

Jaden nodded and headed toward his room. He was pretty disappointed in his own current health status after seeing the physical evidence of what Shane had been talking about. Jaden knew that he'd been told to work on some posture exercises, but he hadn't ever really seen what the good posture was supposed to be, what his bad posture had become, and how it would affect the rest of him. Now he had a damn good idea. He looked down at his good leg.

"You keep working, you hear me," he said to himself. "We need you to stay strong until the other leg can pick up the slack." Because now he started to realize that he really had slack to be picked up. That's probably how his buddy Iain had gotten so big and so strong as he had under Shane's care.

And right now, Jaden was grateful to be under Shane's care himself. He knew the massage coming up wouldn't be the same as sitting in a hot tub and getting gentle pulsing waves of water hitting his back and shoulders, where Jaden was in charge of how close and how hard that water hit him and where it hit him. He winced just at the thought.

But, if a little pain got a lot of gain, he was all for it.

Chapter 4

S EVERAL DAYS LATER Brianna came upon Jaden, sitting outside on the deck with a cup of coffee and a cinnamon bun, watching the birds.

"How are you doing?" she asked, sitting down beside him. She wanted to check him over carefully but didn't want to push the boundaries.

"I'm fine," he said in an offhand way that didn't tell her anything. He stared off into the distance. "I used to bring home every broken and wounded animal possible," Jaden said, pointing out a sparrow that landed on the railing nearby. "From birds to rabbits to squirrels. My foster parents were beside themselves, but I did my best to keep the animals alive and to give them a decent life. I wasn't very successful early on. My foster parents didn't have much money to take the animals to the vet, so I was a constant frustration for them."

"I'm sorry," she said.

"Well, I lost everybody in my birth family at an early age," he said. "And foster homes weren't exactly the same thing. I turned to all the animals as a way to deal with my own losses."

"What happened to your family?"

"Well, my dad took off with my brother," he said with a smile. "That left me with Mom. And my mom was killed in a car accident soon afterward. I don't even know if my dad and my brother knew about her passing, but the police came and put me in foster care, while they tried to find them. The authorities suspected my dad had returned to Germany, and they never did find him in order to let him know about my situation."

She frowned. "Oh my, how sad. Have you tried to contact him since?"

"I haven't found him," he said. "But, then again, I guess I haven't put too much effort into it either."

"No, I guess not," she said. "I'm sure, in that child's heart, it was an act of betrayal."

"It was," he said bitterly. "Definitely abandonment. It doesn't matter if you do split up the kids, one kid to each parent. You shouldn't let go of all contact."

"It's also possible that your dad couldn't have done anything," she said, "in that maybe he passed on too."

"I'd like to think so, and that's terrible of me," he said. "But that's just a reminder how life is always something that you have to adjust to."

"True enough," she said.

"The look on your face says it bothers you more than me."

"Maybe it's because I'm a licensed caregiver. Or female," she said. "I don't know, but it's a betrayal, and I'm not a stranger to that too."

"In what way?" He watched as she hesitated. "Unless it's too private," he said. "I'm not trying to pry."

"It's not that," she said. "It *is* personal, and it is something that I still haven't shared with very many people. But, one of the reasons why I came here and moved in with a girlfriend, even though I had a good job in Houston, was that I was left at the altar by my fiancé." He gasped. She turned and looked at him, then nodded and said, "Right? You read about it happening online. You hear about it from other people, but you never *ever* expect it to be somebody who either you know or, in my case then, who would be me."

"I'm so sorry," he said.

"I'm not," she said. "I mean, it was tough, but it would have been worse if we had married, and then he'd immediately divorced me. Apparently he was sleeping with my maid of honor, and they both forgot to tell me. I believe the two of them have broken up now."

"Wow." He didn't know what to say. When he had asked the question, he realized it was intrusive and probably a little past the point that they were in their friendship, but he had never expected a revelation like that. "I guess the right response would be *Congratulations?*"

She gave a startled laugh. "In what way?"

"That you were saved from a very distressing time of being married to someone who you were sharing with another woman and to later find out that he had betrayed you all along and then jump into a messy and probably expensive divorce. This way, at least, you cut to the chase before it could get any worse. But still, on the day that's supposed to be one of the happiest in your life? ... That's not the place where you want to find out *that*."

"No," she said. "They came to me just before I was due to walk down the aisle."

Her laughter held a note of bitterness that he could fully understand. "I'm very sorry you had to go through that."

"For a long time, I wasn't a very nice person, and I wished all kinds of ill on top of them," she admitted. "I was angry. I was hurt. Now, I'd like to think I have let it go, and I've moved on a bit."

"How long ago was this?"

"Six months," she said in a thoughtful tone, "almost seven now. And the further away I get from that day, the more I realize I didn't really love him. This little inkling had always been inside me that realized something was not quite right. He wasn't the same man who I'd started going out with by the time we were due to walk down the aisle. I figured it was just stress at work, but he stopped sharing things with me and closed himself off a lot."

"Well, obviously he was very conflicted, having gotten himself on two diverging paths that he wasn't happy with."

"Exactly," she said. "And, of course, he hurt a lot of people in the process."

"Yes, indeed."

"And yet the wedding still had to be paid for," she said as she gave another bitter laugh. "A lot of that was on my credit cards. He got to walk away without very much to pay off. His brother was doing the catering for the wedding reception, and I don't know how they worked out that bill between them, but I didn't pay for it. I paid for the church and the minister and the wedding dress, as well as the bridesmaid dresses, including the one my supposed girlfriend was wearing."

He winced at that. "Ouch and double ouch."

She smiled. "And I probably should have shared my tale of woe with more people over time," she said, "because I really do feel better right now. So, thank you for that."

He gave a startled laugh. "Hey, if it makes you feel better, great. I'm just sorry that I asked you and that you had to bring it up here and that you had to actually deal with it back then."

"And, yeah, well, it's better that it's something in my past instead of something to still work on," she said. "I can't imagine it happening to anybody now. As I look back, I realized I should have called him out on all the changes in his personality and tried to figure it all out sooner. But I didn't."

"Hey, communication—true communication—is a two-way street. Why is the onus on you to figure out what your fiancé's story is? Like you said yourself, they both failed to share this with you. Which is why I hate secrets and people who keep them. It's always a selfish motive, serving some selfish purpose for them, that they don't dare speak of or things would change. Your fiancé obviously wanted to keep both you and the other woman. How is that fair to anyone?"

"Yeah, you're right. Plus I was caught up in being happy and getting married and heading toward starting the family I'd always wanted." She gave her head a shake. "But love is blind. And it lets you avoid things that you know are red flags. Things that you should be worried about but aren't yet."

"You do seem to have dealt with it amazingly well at this point, considering that was not even a year ago."

"Well, I didn't think I had, but something is *magical* about this place," she said with a smile.

"It's healing, isn't it?"

"In many ways. And in some other ways that I hadn't really expected," she said, as she waved her arm out at the pastures of green all around the pathways in the gardens. "It's hard to be upset or angry when you can see what people here are really going through, like yourself. And my problems seem very small and insignificant."

"I don't think *small and insignificant* apply in this case," he said in a serious tone, "because they're still huge to you. The fact that you're now capable of talking about it and appear to be ready to move on helps, shows how much you've worked through this. It was a hard blow, and it was a betrayal by somebody who was supposed to be your partner in life. And a second betrayal by a supposed friend." Then he sighed. "It was also a lucky escape."

"And I'll gladly focus on that," she said.

HER WORDS REVERBERATED in Jaden's mind throughout the next few days. They saw each other a few times socially, other than as strictly business appointments of a nurse on his medical team. Jaden and Brianna stopped long enough in their busy lives to have coffee a few times and even managed a meal together here and there. But other than that, his focus had turned inward to healing.

And he understood what she must have gone through for the last six, seven months. He'd been through so much himself, although his accident was over eight months ago. Yet he'd stagnated at the last place. Maybe it was his fault. Maybe he'd realized that this was only as far as he could go, so he had stuffed any hopes away all inside. He would make peace with it, if so. It was the hand he had been dealt, right?

But then he also felt like the previous medical staff had figured that's as far as Jaden would go too. Whereas, like Iain had said, new eyes on Jaden's medical file and his own body had made a huge difference. Shane was looking at this in a completely different manner than Jaden's former PTs had. It wasn't that it was right or wrong. It's just Shane didn't have the same history that Jaden's last center had.

Shane started fresh with Jaden, with no preconceived notions, and Shane also had a different set of skills. And now, five days later, Jaden had slowly begun to retrain his body to sit properly and to listen to his good leg to know when to take a break when needed. And, with Shane's not-easy massages but definitely workable ones, Jaden had found some of his body parts shifting in a much easier flow when he sat, when he stood.

"Have you ever done yoga?" Shane asked Jaden on the Monday after he'd been here for now almost two weeks.

"Yes," he said. "And I quit immediately because men were just not meant to bend into those pretzel shapes."

"Says you," Shane said with a laugh. "Stop thinking about the size of the muscles and start thinking about what the muscles are meant to do."

Jaden just rolled his eyes. "So, what now? You want me to do yoga?"

"It would be a very good idea, but you're not quite there yet. I figure in another six weeks, we'll start you on yoga."

"And the purpose being?"

"Balance, flow, and posture. How's that for a start?"

"I felt sure you'd put flexibility in there."

"Absolutely," Shane said, chuckling. "I forgot that one, didn't I?"

"Yeah," Jaden said. He was surprised to realize he could sit back and relax a little bit more every day.

"At least you're not quite so tense," Shane noted.

"No," he said. "I am starting to relax and to realize that Hathaway House will not gobble me up and eat me whole."

"Is it such a scary place?" Shane asked in surprise.

"Not so much scary but different. And, when you're not whole, change is scary."

Shane stopped, thought about that, and then nodded. "It's one thing for me to face traveling around the world when I'm physically whole," he said. "But I imagine, for you, it's worrying about whether all your needs can be met at every step of the way."

"And how difficult and how challenging and whether I'll physically have the capability or the mentality or have the physical strength or the emotional stability," Jaden added. "I used to travel a lot, and, since my accident, I don't even think I want to travel anywhere now."

"Fear?"

"Potentially," Jaden said, rotating his neck ever-so-slightly to ease up the tension there. Just having this conversation tightened up his neck. And, of course, Shane noticed.

Shane smiled and said, "Let me show you a few different breathing exercises to help release some of that stress you're holding in your neck." By the time they finished those, their session was almost over.

"I meant to ask," Jaden said, "when can I get into that pool?"

"Next week," Shane said.

"Well, that was fast," he said. "I figured I would have to fight you for it."

"No, not at all. But, at one point in time," he said, "everybody gets into the pool, as long as it's something they want or are willing to do. Some people don't like water, but most of the guys I get through here are water bugs."

"Well, that would be me," Jaden said. "Not to mention the euphoric feeling of being weightless and the ease of movement, free from the joint pain."

"Exactly," he said. "It's one of the hardest things to adapt to, finding your body cumbersome and awkward and not moving the way you want it to. Yet you can go into the water, and you're weightless, and everything moves and shifts the way it was meant to. Or at least a little better than otherwise. And then you come back up on land again, and it's a harsh adjustment."

"True enough. If swimming's something I can do though," Jaden said quietly, "I'd like to get into that pool as fast as possible."

Shane studied him for a long moment. "How serious are you? Do you want to start today, or are you willing to wait until next week?"

"Today," he said immediately.

Shane gave a slow and steady nod. "In that case," he said, "I suggest we go see just what your abilities are."

"I was a Navy SEAL," Jaden said with a quirk of his lips. "Water is my home."

"And I've heard that before too," Shane said. "What you used to do and what you can do now are currently two different things."

"Ouch," Jaden said. "Leave me some fantasies, won't you?"

"No," Shane said. "It's all about reality here. And building a whole new future but one that you can achieve."

"Still, let's try the pool now," Jaden said forcefully.

Shane looked at his watch and said, "It's almost lunchtime."

"But my afternoon is all appointments," Jaden said. "Doctors and things. So, we could do the pool now, and then I could have a late lunch and then do my appointments." Shane hemmed and hawed, as if not sure, and Jaden pressed the point. "It's the only way to know what I'll be ready for."

Shane laughed. "Fine, but only if you're at the pool in fifteen minutes."

"Got it," he said. "I'll be there in ten."

And he took off.

Chapter 5

BRIANNA TOOK HER lunch and sat out on the deck. She'd opted for a big chunk of sandwich with as many vegetables as could possibly be packed between two slices of bread, plus a big salad. Dennis had approved and handed her the concoction with a big grin. It had required a skewer to hold it together. She looked at it, shook her head, and said, "I know you think I have a big mouth, Dennis, but ..."

He burst out laughing. "No," he said. "I bet you can squish that down and do real justice to it."

She wasn't so sure, but she now sat outside, well away from the crowd, where she could eat her sandwich and enjoy it in a perfect mess because no way could she eat something like this ladylike. She heard the splashing from the pool down below, but she wasn't in a position to see who was there. She picked up her sandwich, and, by squeezing one corner, she managed to get her mouth around it and took her first bite.

It was absolutely delicious. So she was grateful she'd chosen to eat outside, where nobody could laugh at the dribbles coming down her chin. As it was, she had to secure her napkin around her neck to make sure she preserved her scrubs.

As she ate slowly, she could hear a couple voices calling out, and she cocked her head slightly and realized one of the voices was Jaden. He was talking to Shane. She didn't want to eavesdrop on their conversation, and she was surprised he was still out there and not getting ready for lunch. She had deliberately come early, thinking he would be here too.

Realizing he would not join her now, she shifted slightly so that she could hear a little bit more and wondered what they were up to.

"I told you that I was meant for the water," Jaden said with joy in his voice.

She smiled, loving to hear that. He had a long way to go but apparently had made some significant progress. Iain had left a couple days ago, or at least she thought he had. Then she'd seen him here just about an hour ago. Probably to visit Jaden. She didn't know if Iain had found Jaden or not today. Just as she had wondered about that, she heard a third voice.

"Now, that's what I like to see," he cried out. "All SEALs need to be in the water." There were greetings and cries aplenty at that.

She realized that the men had shifted so that they were closer to the stairs.

"Glad you came back, Iain," Jaden said. "I missed saying goodbye to you."

"Well, the trouble was, I couldn't spend too much time with you when you were adapting," he said, "because you hadn't really sunk into the routines around here. And, once you did, it's almost a personal journey that nobody can help you through."

"And I didn't understand that either before," he said, "but I'm working on it now."

"And that's what you need to do," Iain said. "Put your trust in Shane here, and he'll get you to where you need to be."

"Are you staying for lunch?"

"Yeah, I was thinking of eating with you, but you're still in the pool."

She quit eavesdropping and stared at her sandwich, wishing that she could have gone down there too. But obviously this was bro time. And just then, memories of when she'd had friends to do stuff with too resurfaced. Since she'd arrived, she'd more or less isolated herself into her work and just spent time with Jaden. That probably wasn't a good idea. When she was finally done with her sandwich, she mopped up her chin and tackled her salad.

When she finished and pushed away her plate, a great big tomcat hopped up onto her table and stared at her. She looked at him in surprise. "So, who are you, my friend?" She thought his name was Thomas. But, whatever it was, he was friendly because, as soon as she reached out a hand, his huge guttural engine kicked in, and he wandered closer. She saw his stump, but it didn't appear to bother him in the least.

He batted her softly in the forehead, as if to say, *Hey, more scratching, please.* She reached up to gather him in her arms, groaning slightly at his unexpected weight, and she brought him closer and just cuddled him. This was what she needed. Time with somebody who had no judgment, no opinion as to right or wrong, not asking her if she'd done the right thing or had done more of something else.

She hadn't realized how much her life had been generated by other people's opinions, other people's comments, other people's expectations, rather than her own expectations. She hadn't done anything wrong, but she truly needed to focus on her own needs and wants now. She'd taken time to adjust to her new job and to her new apartment and to her new city. She needed some time to just *be* here, not stuck in her mind, not reliving her wedding fiasco and the months that followed.

Luckily she'd found one person to be friendly with here. Surely having Jaden as a friend was a good first step. At least this furry guy appeared to think so. Thomas reached up with a paw and batted her chin ever-so-slightly. She lowered it, and he almost bit her, but his nip was soft and gentle. She looked at him in surprise. "What do you want?" She reached up and chucked him under the chin several times, scratching gently. His eyes almost crossed with pleasure. She chuckled out loud.

And then an older man spoke to her.

She opened her eyes to see the Major, somebody she'd only seen once, where he had formally introduced himself.

He stared at her with a big grin on his face. "At least Thomas had the manners to wait until you finished eating," he said. He reached out a hand and said, "I believe we met earlier. Forgive me for not remembering your name. You're one of the new ones here."

"About six weeks now," she confirmed, nodding. "I'm Brianna."

He nodded. "I'm the Major, Dani's father."

She grinned. "And apparently the animal caretaker, from what I hear."

"Well, I also play a mean game of chess, and I can cheat fairly well at checkers, and I'm pretty poor at the pool table, but I do enjoy a game every now and again."

She smiled. "Is this guy yours?"

"Well, he belongs to Hathaway House," the Major corrected. He motioned at a nearby chair. "May I?"

"Sure," she said with a bright smile. "I was just thinking that I haven't really had a chance to get to know too many people yet."

"Except I noticed you've been spending some time with Jaden," he said with a knowing smirk.

Heat flushed up her cheeks. "That obvious, huh?"

"A little bit," he said, "but I'm a romantic at heart."

She rolled her eyes at him. "It's not like that."

"It absolutely is like that," he said. "At least, it's the start of something like that."

"Well, a start is one thing," she said, "but we're a long way away from anything other than just being two new people who bonded."

"And sometimes it's just as simple as that," he said with a smile.

"Maybe," she said. "And maybe not."

Just then, the cat in her arms jumped up onto the table and headed toward the Major. He chuckled, then patted his chest, and the cat jumped down, expecting his human to catch him. And, indeed, the Major did.

"Obviously he's used to you," she said, laughing at the way the cat just totally spread out, looking for cuddles.

"Most of them understand affection. Most of them understand trust. It's only after we have betrayed that trust that they get edgy. But they're quite likely to trust the next person."

"Unlike people," she said soberly. "We lose trust in one, and we tend to judge every other one the same way."

"Isn't that the truth," he said sadly. His gray eyes were penetrating as they studied her. "There was a note of personal truth in that statement too."

"I'm sure everybody here has a story," she said, laughing.

"We all do," he confirmed. "And the person I was ten years ago is a very different person from who I am now."

"In what way?" she asked curiously.

His eyes lit up. "Because you're new," he said with a wink, "you haven't heard *all* the stories about me. But I was a very angry war vet. My body wasn't working, and my heart was sure that the world had forsaken me. My soul was more than ready to jump off this planet and take a plunge into whatever came after this. I was suicidal, depressed, and certain that the world had forgotten me."

"I'm so sorry," she said gently. "Nothing quite like those kinds of feelings, is there?"

"No," he said. "The only thing that kept me going was Dani. She wouldn't give up on me."

"She's very special," Brianna said.

"Dani is definitely a special person. But she's who she is also because of what I put her through," he said sadly. "If I could go back in time and change it, I would."

"Maybe she wouldn't want that," Brianna said quietly. "Maybe she understands how much better she is now. Plus, together you two created this masterpiece out of that chaos. So something very magical and wonderful came out of that hardship."

He nodded. "And you might want to apply that logic to yourself," he said with a twinkle in his eye. "Not sure what the darkness is in your life, but it's there. I approached you because you are still giving off this I-want-to-be-alone signal, telling people to stay away."

She looked at him in surprise. "I wondered about that," she said. "I figured it was me and my insecurities, not wanting to join other people."

"Except for Jaden," the Major interrupted, followed by a wink.

"Except for Jaden," she repeated, nodding her agreement. "But I'm always at a table alone. And, when I turn around, I see everybody else with full tables."

"Often I don't think we're really aware of how others perceive us," he said with a chuckle. He started to stand up, and the big cat jumped onto the table once more. "Looks like Thomas wants to stay with you. I'll go grab something to eat."

"Well, I had Dennis make me a sandwich," she said. "It was delicious."

"Good," he said. "Maybe I'll grab one myself." He stopped as he walked past the table, then looked down at her and said, "Maybe, if you just feel a little easier about that problem inside, you'll find other people approaching you."

She sat back and thought about it. She glanced around and realized that seriously every table was full except hers. She had come and approached Jaden that day not too long ago, and the two of them had clung together. Yet, without him, here she was, alone.

Was she still putting up walls and pushing people away because of what happened with her fiancé? Is that really how she wanted people to perceive her now? She groaned, picked up her dishes, and walked them over to one of the big carousels where they placed all the dirty dishes. Then she refilled her coffee, called to Thomas to follow her, and walked downstairs to see the other animals.

Instead of going to the pool—because she could already feel herself not being welcome there because Iain was with Jaden for a visit of their own, and that was a time that she knew Jaden really wanted—so she headed inside to the vet's office.

The receptionist looked up, smiled, and asked, "May I help you?"

Self-consciously, Brianna shrugged and said, "This is the first time I've been down here. I'm Brianna, a new nurse upstairs, and I've been here about six weeks but have yet to make my way down. Only Thomas came to visit me over my lunch hour, and he reminded me that I had yet to make everybody's acquaintance down here."

The woman looked at her, then Thomas, and smiled and said, "Well, you picked a great time. It's empty right now."

And, true enough, as Brianna looked around the reception area, she saw no patients or animals. "You often get quiet times like this?"

"Almost never," the woman said cheerfully. "And I'm Sherry," she said, pointing to her name tag. "You probably know Stan, our resident vet already."

"I have met Stan, yes. Are there any animals to visit with?"

"Well, there are always the ones outside," she said. "We have a massive rabbit that I'm about to take out and put into a pen. We've been working on his special place for the last week or so. Iain came back today and was bringing the enclosures and a trapdoor to put in. Come follow me and see for yourself."

With a smile, Brianna walked outside with Sherry to see a rabbit that had to be on steroids. "Oh, my gosh," she said. "He's huge." His pen wasn't finished yet. It was clearly open on one end. However, the bunny seemed to be content to stay right here, beside what had to be Iain.

"He's also a big baby," Sherry said. "Iain is here right now, completing this run."

Brianna nodded, noting the man was installing some hardware. "Does this give the rabbit his own pen now?"

Iain nodded and turned to face the women. "His own

pen and his own hutch and his own access to the vet clinic," he said. "So he can come inside and outside on his own, and yet he's safe to do so alone. That way the clinic staff are freed up a little more."

Iain had inset a pet door into an existing side door, for the rabbit to come and go. They probably had to get a large doggie door to accommodate this fluffy rabbit. Brianna wondered how much of him was deceptive fluff and how much was true poundage. Regardless, now he had his own run. "That'll make for a happy rabbit."

"Gets him outside into the fresh air and gives him fresh green grass too."

"At least for the moment," Brianna said with a frown. She had some serious doubts as to how long any allotted grass would last with this fellow around to eat it up. "I get the feeling this guy can eat it up in no time."

"We'll split up this run of his in a little bit," he said. "It's along a fence, so we can keep going as long as we need to. But we are putting some offshoot runs in as well, so we can section off areas as needed to recover the grass, if the rabbit eats too much."

"*If?*" Brianna repeated. "From the size of him," she said in astonishment, "I imagine he'll eat a ton."

He grinned up at her. "I'm Iain."

She smiled and said, "You weren't on my roster, but I'm one of the new nurses, Brianna. I started just a bit before you left."

He nodded and said, "Nice to meet you. How are you enjoying this place?"

"It's such an interesting system here," she said. "We get first-hand relationships with some of the patients, when we're part of their medical team, but we miss out on some others. Like I did with you."

"Exactly," he said. Then he looked at the rabbit. "Anyway, this guy's name is Hoppers." He stepped into the pen and reached down, then scooped out the great big rabbit.

She watched his prosthetic limb bending and holding him easily. "That prosthetic looks pretty cool," she said.

"It is. I came in to get a couple adjustments made here, as this one is new to me. A group of friends of mine have quite the prosthetic designer with them in New Mexico, and I had this one commissioned."

"Is that titanium?"

"Stainless steel with some robotics involved, but, all in all, it's a heck of an improvement over the peg leg I had previously." And he laughed at that. "Obviously it wasn't a wooden peg leg, but it wasn't a whole lot better either."

"Well, I'm happy for you," she said. "It looks stunning, and it's remarkably mobile."

He held out his arms, filled with the mondo rabbit, and asked, "Do you want to say hi?"

She reached over and gently rubbed the rabbit's nose. "I figured you'd be visiting with Jaden."

"He's gone to a couple of his appointments," Iain said easily.

She nodded. "I thought he was at the pool."

"He was. We'll meet up later," he said. "I'll be here for the day, while I work on fixing this up."

"Lucky Hoppers here." She gently stroked the superlong ears to go with the supersize giant rabbit. He must have been a hefty armload for Iain to carry, but he didn't appear to be in any stress over it. "I gather he's now a permanent resident?" she asked, looking back at Sherry.

She shrugged. "We have a lot of those, so why not one

more?" At that, a small dog came out on wheels. "This is Racer. Generally we keep him fairly close with us because he can get into trouble with his wheels."

"Like what trouble?"

Iain laughed. "I caught him going up the stairs, dragging the wheels behind him, but, when he got to the very top, there were people. So, he was stuck with his wheels under the lip. We managed to free up the wheels and get him safely to the top floor. It's much easier if he uses the ramp, but he's stubborn."

"That's because he probably doesn't realize he has a disability," Brianna said with a laugh.

"Isn't that the truth."

Sherry excused herself, taking Racer with her, and left them to touch base with Stan and the clinic's waiting room.

Brianna could feel something in Iain's gaze. She looked up at him and raised an eyebrow. "Something bothering you?"

"Nope," he said, "but Jaden and I are good friends, and he told me how you and him have been spending a lot of time together."

"When our schedules allow, yes," she agreed with a laugh. "He's a nice guy," she said, wondering if something else was behind that penetrating gaze of Iain's.

"He is. He's also honest and loyal and honorable."

Her cheeks warmed up immediately. "He told you about my history, huh?"

He shrugged. "In a place like this, everybody has a history. But he did mention that you had an issue from your past."

"Yeah. I just had the Major bring up another issue connected to that one too." She groaned. "It's hard to think everybody knows."

"Not everybody knows anything," he said. "Jaden shared with me, knowing I won't tell anyone else. And the Major is very astute. So is Dani. So, if you're hiding anything, you can count on her finding it out."

"Yeah," Brianna said, "but she already knows. I explained my situation before she hired me and how I wanted to make a fresh start here."

"And the Major is a people person, so, when he finds certain ones off on their own or doing something that he would feel was antisocial, he'll get right in there and help you out of your shell."

"I didn't think I had one," she said.

"Well, you won't after you're here a few more months," he said, chuckling. "I can guarantee you that."

"I felt comfortable from the very first with Jaden," she said. "My walls weren't up, as the Major pointed out earlier today. Jaden and I were both new here at approximately the same time, and that seemed to give us some common ground."

"Indeed." Iain smiled and slowly lowered himself and the great big rabbit to the ground. Hoppers didn't appear to care one way or the other. He moved around, sniffling and checking out the grass in his new pen. She and Iain stood and watched as Hoppers explored all that newly opened-up space just for him.

On the far side of the fence, two horses arrived. She looked at them, smiled, and said, "Wow. This is such a special place."

Iain immediately stepped closer and reached out a hand and gently brushed the midnight-black horse's nose. The horse lifted up his head, obviously looking for an under-the-chin scratch. Iain chuckled and gently stroked the neck and the jaws of the beautiful horse. "This is Midnight," he said. "He's Dani's personal horse, but he's a big baby."

She shifted so that she could walk up on the side and gently introduced herself to the horse. "I've never been around animals of this size," she murmured. "It's a little intimidating."

"Since my childhood in Kentucky, I've loved horses," Iain said. "I love all animals. You could say they were my first love. Then it was the navy."

"More similarities that you have with Jaden."

"Yep," he said. "Both of us are good people."

"I'll try to remember that."

"Do that," he said. "He's a good man."

With that, she gave a half smile and a wave and turned and walked toward her apartment. She needed a few moments by herself after the Major and now Iain had seen through her "shell" to see her soft vulnerable part. She thought she had locked that hurt down. She thought she had been putting on a brave front while she dealt with those sad memories that still seemed to pop up at work or when she was lonely in a crowd or other inopportune times. Not like she could control them. Or at least she hadn't been able to yet.

But they were easier and easier to dismiss now. She knew she and her ex were not well suited. Not for the long run obviously. And now that she had met Jaden, she realized how little she and Gerald had shared of each other's lives, even at the very beginning of their relationship. *How sad*. They had no true communication. And, yes, she wasn't just commenting on his affair with her maid of honor. They really didn't talk, not like she and Jaden talked. When Jaden speaks to her, he's coming from his heart. And he's this big Navy SEAL, a wounded warrior—neither of which her ex could claim to be.

So if Jaden could open up and could lay himself bare to her, why couldn't Gerald? She sighed. No matter. He would never be acceptable in her eyes. She had a new bar to measure her next relationship by. *Jaden.* And she wouldn't accept less.

So she was a little shocked to hear the Major addressing her "shell" and now Iain speaking about her obvious distrust that still lingers within her. And here she hadn't thought she had been putting out any *stay away* signs. Yet, according to both of them—and all in the last hour too—obviously, to them, she was.

Also it sounded like Iain was promoting Jaden as being a good person. She already knew that, but still she wasn't in the market. At least not for a while. That last attempt had been more than enough for her.

THE SHORT VISIT with Iain during a PT session had been great, but now Jaden wanted to get to his room for a shower so he could meet up with Iain during his downtime and spend some time with his friend. Jaden was in a completely different mind-set than when he'd first arrived. Because originally he'd been afraid that all this hoopla was for naught and that his friend was delusional. But now that Jaden saw what Shane had showed him and how far down that road to recovery that Iain himself had gotten, well, that was a whole different story. As Jaden escaped from his last appointment, he pulled out his phone and texted his buddy. **You still**

here?

Yep. Come on down to the pen and take a look at Hoppers.

Jaden grinned and, using his wheelchair, took the elevator down and outside. There, the great big rabbit was sprawled on its side, out in the fresh grass. "And the hardware worked?"

"Sure did. Look at that guy. I also put dividers in one part of the pen so that they could close off part of the run to help the grass recover."

"What about fresh water?"

"He has water inside his pen," he said. "It's already automatically plumbed."

"Wow, that's fancy," he said.

"Well, this guy can probably live about seven years or so. He's only a year old now."

"Is he even full-grown?" Jaden asked in fascination.

"I think so," Iain said, "just like the rest of us here, we really don't know when the growth stops, do we?"

"I don't think it ever stops," he said. "I think it's a case of full speed ahead all the time."

"I met your girlfriend," Iain said.

Jaden looked at him in surprise. "Did Brianna come down here?"

"Yes. I also heard her up on the lunchroom deck with the Major. She looked a little bit disoriented, but the Major can have that effect on people."

"It's funny," Jaden said. "I see her as really friendly and outgoing, but I'm not seeing other people having the same relationship or interaction with her."

"Yeah. It's all the walls that she keeps up," Iain said, looking down at the rabbit, then he smiled at his buddy.

"But she has doors for you to get in and out."

"Is that a good thing?" Jaden asked.

"I don't know," Iain said with an intense look and an even bigger smile. "Maybe that's a question you should answer."

"It's a good thing as far as I'm concerned," he said carefully, "but only if it's a two-way street."

"And that's why she's got walls for the other people, and the doors are for you—because it's definitely two-way."

Chapter 6

I N THE BACK of her mind, Brianna knew she was waiting until she saw Jaden again.

Dani came to the doorway of Brianna's office and studied her.

"Problems?" Brianna asked in a light tone.

Dani shook her head. "Just wondering if you need a meeting to see how you're getting on. See how you've adapted?"

"Well, I guess I've been here about six weeks," she said with a smile. "So, if you feel like we need a meeting, I'm good with it."

"How are you getting along with the people?"

At that, Brianna sat back in her chair, studied Dani, and said, "Did you want me to come to your office?"

Dani gave a nod. "Good idea. Let's make this official."

She quickly closed the folders she was working on, then picked up her cup of coffee, and followed Dani back to her office. There, behind closed doors, she said, "Do you have a reason to ask about me getting along with people?"

"It's part of my overall worry," Dani said with a half laugh. "A lot of people are here, and personality differences show up."

"I don't think I've had trouble with anyone yet," she said. Only now she wondered why Dani had brought it up.

"Just a couple mentions were made to me," Dani said quietly. "That you appeared to be very reserved and a loner."

"Ah," Brianna said, staring off in the distance, nodded, a little hurt. "You're right. I probably am."

"Still afraid of getting hurt?"

"Not consciously, no," she said, "but I have noticed that, when I go out to the general public areas here, I tend to be the only one at my table."

"Those walls are pretty hard to let go of, aren't they?"

"And do people know that instinctively?" Brianna asked, puzzled. "Do they look at me and say, *Oh, wow, she looks like she's in a bad mood. I better stay away?*"

At that, Dani burst out laughing. "No, not at all," she said. "But I think it's a case of, when there are two places open, you do tend to give off this stay-away vibe. So they instinctively go to the other place."

"Sounds like the same thing to me," Brianna said with a sigh. "And here I had thought I was handling this so well. That I was projecting this happy, serene expression while I work through the remaining memories. I swear I thought I had this under control." She frowned at Dani. Not *at Dani* but at the fact that Brianna had failed so miserably to conceal her lingering pain. *Plus* this felt like a psychotherapy session. Even with Dani, it felt invasive. No wonder Jaden hated them so. Brianna shook her head, gathering her thoughts. *What had she just said to Dani? Oh, yeah …* "I wasn't thinking that my past relationship was basically telling everybody to keep out, but maybe that is what I'm doing."

"Well, at least you're open about it," Dani said, with a knowing smile.

"I'm trying to be."

"Do you get along with anyone?"

"If you're asking about Jaden, then you might as well ask," she said. "I'm obviously an open book, unbeknownst to me. Everybody else seems to be asking."

"Okay. I'm asking," Dani's grin split wide and grew infectious.

"Honestly, when we first arrived, we were both new," she said. "I think we gravitated together maybe because we each recognized a newbie, that new kid at school. I forgot to put up the walls, or maybe Jaden wouldn't have regarded them as walls anyway. I don't know."

"He came here not really as a last resort but more as a case of he might as well try our rehab system here, yet he didn't really expect anything much, I think," Dani said. "I'm pretty sure he came based on Iain's recommendation as it was."

"Yes, and he has really enjoyed seeing his buddy back here. The fact that Iain came to visit yesterday was huge."

"And I think they'll probably spend more time together too because Iain will remain in town. He's also pretty handy with a hammer and nails and has done a few small jobs for us."

"Which is good for him too," she said. "There's such a vast difference between the two men though."

"In what way?"

"Their physical fitness, for one," Brianna said.

"When he first arrived, Iain was in the same shape as Jaden. But he has come a long way."

Brianna stared at her in surprise. "Really?"

"Yes," Dani said with a smile. "Like I said, Iain has come a long way."

"He has, indeed."

"That's what's given Jaden so much hope that he can

have the same success." Dani focused on Brianna, watching her expressions.

Inside, Brianna wondered if that was true, or if Dani was slightly exaggerating. "I'm not sure Jaden has that same potential to grow his leg back that big."

"Maybe his genetics might hold him back, but he can still grow a lot bigger and stronger than what he is now. And it's not about size. It's about strength, flexibility, and health."

"Exactly," she said. "I wonder if that comparison is hard on him. Seeing his friend doing so well, and yet he's not."

"Possibly, for the here and now, but it should also be encouraging to Jaden to realize he can come that far too."

Brianna nodded, wondering at another thought that came through her mind. But it was a little too horrible to contemplate. She frowned and looked down at her fingers.

"Problems?"

Not wanting to share at this point in time, Brianna smiled, shook her head, and said, "Dennis is very friendly."

"Dennis likes to know everyone here," Dani said. "He's been with me for years. Right from the beginning in fact."

"Not only does he run a great kitchen," she said, "but he always seems to remember what I've eaten and what I should be eating." She laughed, but it was stilted.

"That's because he cares," Dani said seriously.

"I think everybody here does," Brianna said in bewilderment. "How did you find such a great collection of these very skilled people and pull them together like this?"

"I'm not sure," Dani said, "but you can bet I'm trying to maintain it."

"Well, you don't have to worry about me," Brianna said, ready to make her exit but remaining in her seat. She wasn't sure if there was another reason behind Dani's questions or not, but she wanted to set her boss at ease. "I really enjoy being here. I'm enjoying the atmosphere, the healing, just everything about the center. You've built yourself quite a place. You should be proud of your accomplishments."

Dani nodded. "I am," she said. "It's been a very long journey to this point. But, just like I see the progress of my own father and all the patients around here, it's amazing how much that same growth, optimism, and positivity works outward to everybody else around us."

"Like you and me?"

"Exactly," Dani said with a half laugh. She looked at her watch and said, "And it's lunchtime. Are you up for joining me?"

"Sure," she said. "I have no clue if Jaden is ready for lunch or not."

Dani added, "It'd be easy enough to join him."

On that note, the two of them got up and headed toward the cafeteria.

"How do you decide when animals get to stay here?"

"Stan has a certain budget to stick to, so I get his feedback," she said. "One of the difficulties is some of the animals have very long lifespans, so we have to take that into account. For example, the horses. But, as I already have my own horses that I keep here," she said with a tender smile as she looked outside, "it's pretty easy to take in a few others that need help."

"I was thinking of the cats and dogs and Hoppers, I guess, is his name."

"Isn't he a huge rabbit?"

"He's massive," Brianna said in surprise. "And he's got such a great temperament."

"Exactly. He's a pretty easy addition for this place."

"We could set up a petting zoo," Brianna said with a laugh.

"Ugh," Dani said. "I like people just fine, but I'm not sure I want to bring in curiosity seekers. Feels like that would change the healing energy of our place."

"Oh, good point," she said. "I guess all of us here prefer our privacy."

"That's the thing about a center like this," she said. "You fit in here. Every broken soul knows there's a place for them at Hathaway House. And, while they're here, they slowly start to put the pieces of themselves back together again. Not just physically but it's the emotional and the mental and the almost soulful levels that people have to heal. It's a complete process in order to be whole, figuratively, regardless of the condition of the physical body. These individuals come here as patients, looking to get their bodies back, but they don't realize it doesn't happen unless all the parts and pieces come together in unity. And that goes for the staff too."

Out in the hallway was a commotion, then somebody called for Dani. She looked at Brianna and said, "Duty calls. I'll see you later." And she headed off down the hallway to where somebody stood outside a patient's room, leaving Brianna to her thoughts.

Except her thoughts were totally eclipsed by one bigger thought that couldn't be true. Could it?

"THAT WAS A great day," Shane said, as he helped Jaden to sit back up again.

Jaden sat in his wheelchair, literally shaking. "Says you," he said. "My body is so done."

"Hot tub?"

Jaden looked at Shane in surprise and then nodded slow-ly. "That might just be the answer. Let's go then," he said, and Shane stepped up behind him and grabbed a couple towels off the shelves, then dropped them into his lap and wheeled him toward the elevator. Jaden hated to say it, but he was so very glad that Shane pushed the wheelchair because Jaden wasn't sure his arms would get him very far.

But the thought of being in the hot tub or even in the pool first? … Either would work as his body continued to shake inside and outside. It was embarrassing, but it was also evidence of a truly hard workout. For that, he was proud of what he had accomplished this session. As the two of them hit the lower level, Jaden took several deep breaths to calm his body further before he faced anybody else here. "Any chance of the pool first?"

"Absolutely," Shane said. He walked Jaden up to the closest pool edge, braked the wheelchair alongside the crystal blue water, and said, "I'll take the towels. You just go in."

Jaden had worn a muscle shirt and shorts for his PT, but now he took off the sweaty muscle shirt and tossed it to the tiled surround of the pool and grasped the railing that led to the ladder into the pool and by the steps of the shallow end. He stood from his wheelchair, still with some residual shakiness, and, rather than even trying to take any steps or to make a graceful entrance, he just fell in over the side into the pool.

As soon as the water closed over his head, he groaned. He waited until he was out of air before slowly rising to the surface, floating. It was all he could do. He saw Shane watching him as he broke through the surface. He just smiled and said, "I'm fine, but I sure as heck am not going to move much. Yet the water feels great."

"Was the session today that bad?"

"No, not necessarily," he said, "but you pushed me hard, and I am exhausted."

"Good," Shane said. "So let's see how you feel after you get back out again."

"I figured I'll stay here for a bit."

"And miss lunch?"

"I can't afford to miss lunch," he said. "I'm always hungry these days."

Shane looked at him in surprise, then grabbed his notebook from his pocket and wrote down something. "You need to tell me things like that," he said.

Jaden rolled over in the water, then looked up at him and said, "I didn't think that was important."

"It's very important," he said. "What are you typically eating?"

"Protein," he said. "I'm always craving protein."

Shane nodded and wrote something else down.

"Don't tell me that's wrong too?"

"No, not wrong at all," Shane said. "It's important you get enough protein while you're building muscles. But we also want to make sure that you're getting a lot of vegetables too, so you're not lacking nutrients."

"And cake and ice cream are nutrients, right?"

"Not quite," Shane said with a laugh. He looked over, assessing Jaden. "Will you make it to lunch?"

"I just said so," he said, a little irritated at having to repeat himself, at having Shane questioning his mobility right now.

"Or do you want me to get Dennis to bring you something?"

The thought almost stopped him in his tracks. That would be so much nicer. So much easier. "Would he?"

"Sure, he would," Shane said. "If you want to stay in the water and work some of those muscles, just make sure you do ten minutes in the hot tub too."

"I think I could manage that." He thought about it, nodded, and said, "Actually I'd really appreciate it if Dennis would deliver my meal. The thought of having to get up, get changed, go in for lunch, and then return to my room …" He just shook his head, wordless.

"Exactly what I was thinking," Shane said. "Let me go talk to him."

"Although I don't know what lunch is," Jaden said, suddenly realizing he may not get what he wanted for lunch. Shane just lifted a hand as he took the stairs to the dining area deck. Too late for Jaden to even make a suggestion. Maybe that was for the best. As he knew already, Dennis was always looking after everybody's nutritional values anyway. So Jaden was worrying for no good reason.

He stayed and floated in the water, absolutely loving it, until he got a little chilled. Then, instead of using his wheelchair or crab-walking, Jaden crossed the cement on his butt and slipped into the nearby hot tub. As soon as he did, shivers racked his soul, and he realized just how chilled he'd gotten. He immediately sank until just his face showed, letting his body warm up.

It was one of the oddities of sunshine and pools, that, at one point in time, your body did cool to the point that you just couldn't stay in the water.

"That's a heck of a picture," a man said.

Jaden opened his eyes to see Dennis standing here, his hands on his hips, studying Jaden.

He rose up out of the water and sat a little higher up on the steps in the hot tub. "I caught a chill," he confessed.

Immediately Dennis's smile disappeared. He shook his head. "You know what happens when you overdo it, right?"

"Don't tell Shane, please," Jaden begged in a teasing manner. "I promise I'll be good. But I don't want Shane to take the pool away from me."

"I can see that," Dennis said. "So, I would have just served you up something, but I figured, since we had such a wide variety today, that I might as well come and ask you what you wanted."

When he listed off the reams of food choices, Jaden was stunned. "Is it a special day today?"

"In a way," he said. "Dani's got a bunch of investors and doctors and whatnot coming and walking through the place."

"Well, all of the food sounds wonderful," he said. "I don't even know what to ask for."

"Do you trust me?" Dennis asked as he turned away and headed for the stairs.

"Absolutely, but I'm starved."

"I've heard that a time or two," he said. "Back in ten."

Dennis was a man of his word, so Jaden knew to just relax and wait on his meal. He sat on the edge of the hot tub, wondering if it was safe for him to make his way over to one of the lounges in the sun to stay warm. He looked at it, then calculated the distance between it and the hot tub ... and groaned.

Just then, a female spoke. "How about I move one of the chairs in closer?"

He shifted to see Brianna standing nearby, holding a cup of coffee in one hand and a piece of cake in the other. He grinned at her. "Did you just read my mind?"

"Nope, but I heard Dennis speaking with you," she said. "So, if you don't mind, I thought I'd bring my dessert and join you."

"You're always welcome. You know that," he said. He looked over at the lounge chairs. "I think the sun will be too hot, yet I don't want to get cold either."

"So," she said, "I'll give you these to hold," and she reached down and gave him her plate and her cup, and he held them easily and watched her, as she grabbed two loungers and brought them between the pool and the hot tub in the semishade. Then she walked back over, accepted her cup and plate back, and sat down on the chaise farther away.

He hitched his butt over a few feet and made his way up into the chair. "Thank you," he said. "That made life that much easier."

"You were looking a little tired," she said.

"Just a little? Then I'm doing pretty good," he said. "Both Shane and Dennis have been on my case this morning."

"And how's it going?"

"I guess I'm seeing progress," he said. "And Iain's visit was great."

"Ah, Iain," she said, with a nod, as if that explained everything.

He looked at her curiously. "You met him, didn't you?"

"I did," she said. "It's remarkable. He's looking so fit and healthy. And he had that crazy techno prosthetic."

"Right. Isn't that all amazing?" he said. "I don't know that I can get quite as good or quite as strong or quite as fit as Iain, but he's my benchmark. *Wow.* I want to get as close to all that as I can."

Chapter 7

B RIANNA DID WORRY about how much Iain's success affected Jaden's own hoped-for outcome but knew that she couldn't really say anything to him about tempering his hopes a bit. The last thing she wanted to do was be a downer, raining on his parade, stalling his progress in any way. "I'm sure you'll do your utmost best," she said warmly.

"And the question is whether that'll be good enough, right?" His mood appeared to dim along with his smile.

"Not at all," she said, sitting up and throwing her legs over the chaise to face Jaden. "It's important that you stay positive and hopeful and give it your all because I don't think *anybody* knows how much we can do for ourselves until we just give ourselves permission to go after what we want, to stay out of our own way."

"Of course. I agree," he said, "and I really want to get where Iain is. I guess he felt doubts like this along the way to where he is now too."

Brianna nodded. "Yes, ask Iain about his doubts and what pushed him through those. I bet some successes here have even surprised Shane."

At that, Jaden quirked one eyebrow up, considering. "Yeah, I bet so."

Just then Dennis came down the stairs with a large tray.

Jaden sat up and accepted the tray, staring at the double

plates, and said, "Man, this looks divine."

"Well, you've got protein and veggies on one and a salad on the other," he said, as he walked over and picked up a small little coffee table from the big patio area and put it beside Jaden. "So, you can eat one at the time, and that'll get some of your nutritional requirements in for the day."

"You think?" Jaden joked. "A ton of food is here."

"If it's too much, just say so," he said, "and I'll take something back."

"You could take back the salad?"

"Nope. The only thing I'll take back is some of that fried chicken."

"In that case," Jaden said, "I'll do my best to get it all down."

"Good enough," he said. He looked over at Brianna. "Did you have enough?"

"I did," she said. "Thank you."

He nodded, then turned and left.

"It's hard to imagine this over-and-beyond service at any other place. And Dennis's attitude is the best," Jaden said. "You've probably worked in different places. Have you ever seen anything like this?"

"No, this is definitely a unique scenario," she said. "And the places that I did work in were not like this, where everybody is working to improve themselves. My previous positions weren't at rehab centers. Some were long-term care facilities. I worked in several geriatric units, and they were all interesting and different in their own right. But not much hope was had in those facilities. So I'm so much happier to be here, watching all of you work miracles."

"Yep." Jaden nodded. "We're all miracles in progress around here."

By the time he finished his huge meal, he looked at her and said, "You know what? I was tired before I started eating, but now I'm exhausted."

She looked at him in concern. "Do you want a hand to get back to your room?"

He hesitated. It went against everything inside him to ask her for help. Finally he bolstered his pride—or probably had to shut it down—and said, "Could you at least bring my wheelchair over here?"

She nodded, hopped to her feet, walked over, and brought his wheelchair up to his side. She held it as he made the transition from the lounge into his chair. When he finally collapsed into it, she said, "I'll take you up to your room."

"I'm not that bad off."

"It doesn't matter if you're that bad or not," she said. "I'm still a nurse, and I'd hate to see anybody suffering needlessly." She wasn't sure if she'd insulted him with that, but she moved him steadily toward the elevator. By the time she got him back to his room, he was a little stiff-necked and detached.

He nodded his thanks and said, "Close the door on your way out, will you?"

She took the hint and stepped outside, closing the door. Then she walked outside and collected all the dishes onto the tray and carried them up the stairs. She met Dennis outside on the dining area deck, as he wiped off tables.

She said, "He did pretty well."

Dennis looked at the empty plates, smiled, and said, "He did very well." He glanced over the railing toward the pool and the hot tub. "Where is he now?"

"Gone to bed," she said. "His words were," and she

quoted, "*I was tired before I ate, but now I'm exhausted.*"

Dennis nodded. "A big meal can do that." He took the tray and the dishes, then thanked her kindly.

She turned and headed back through the cafeteria toward her office. Her revelation while she had been sitting with Dani this morning was something Brianna needed to peruse. It was an ugly, ugly thought. And she didn't want it to be true, but something was cooking in the back of her mind that made her wonder if she was choosing to be friendly with Jaden because of his disability. To build a friendship and potentially more than that because of his disability.

Where had that come from? That was such an ugly thought that she didn't know how to wrap her mind around it. Because what possible motivation could be behind it? The trouble was, she already knew the answer to that.

Because Jaden wouldn't likely have a ton of women who he would go off with and betray her.

She could feel the tears collecting in her eyes as she headed to her office. She wiped them away surreptitiously so that nobody saw.

Back at her desk, she brought up a Word document and just typed out all the craziness in her head, as if she could permanently dispel it from her brain. *Like that could happen.* Was she really such a small-minded person who would deliberately focus her attention on somebody who was struggling to become more normal because Brianna figured she'd have no competition or because he would have less options and wouldn't likely betray her? It was such an awful thing to think that she could hardly fight her way through this.

She quickly whispered, "God, I hope not."

Shane popped his head around the corner and said, "Are you talking to me?"

She immediately shook her head. "No," she said, "I'm not."

His face darkened as he studied her. "Looks like you need to talk to somebody."

She shook her head. "No, no, no, no," she said. "Some things are just not meant to be voiced out loud."

At that, he deliberately refused to leave her.

She groaned and said, "I just came up with something that's pretty … inane, or maybe just totally insane, and I'm hoping it's not true."

"Interesting," Shane said. "Maybe you should talk to me."

"It's not that easy," she said.

"It never is, but chances are it's got to do with Jaden. In which case, I really would like to know."

"No," she said. "It's too ugly. I keep hoping I'm wrong."

"Is it about you or about him?"

"Both," she said, with a broken laugh. She looked down at her computer, quickly deleted the document she had just typed up—God forbid anybody find it—and said, "I think I'll take a half day off." She stood, and her hands were shaking.

Immediately Shane reached out, grabbed her hands, held them together, and said, "Calm down, and let's talk this through. I don't know what's going on, but you need a friend right now."

She looked at him, haunted. "I'm not sure I deserve to have any friends," she whispered.

She broke free and raced out, leaving Shane staring behind her.

WHEN HE WOKE up later that afternoon, Jaden realized he'd already missed one appointment. He groaned and managed to get into the wheelchair, then headed for his second afternoon appointment. As he rolled down the hallway, Shane stood there, waiting for him. "You're not my next appointment," he said. "What's up?"

"Did anything happen with you and Brianna at noon today?"

He shook his head. "Not really. I got extremely tired. Dennis brought food, and I got even more tired after I ate, so she helped me back to my room. Why?"

Shane frowned. "She just seemed really upset afterward," he said. "She has taken the afternoon off."

"Interesting," he said. "Well, I hope she's okay. I'm late for an appointment, but I'll check in with her afterward."

"The thing is," Shane said, "it'd be best if you don't. I'm not sure what's going on, but it's something she needs to work out for herself."

Jaden nodded and said, "Maybe she just needs a friend."

"I think she's been very short on those for a long time," Shane said, staring off in the distance.

"Well, after what happened to her, it's no wonder," Jaden said.

"Is it something you can tell me?"

"I think several people know. It's not like it's a big secret, but I'm sure she doesn't want everyone to know either," he said, hesitating.

"Well, I'd like to know so that maybe I can help her."

How could Jaden say no to that? He studied Shane's earnest face and nodded. "I understand. I'm only passing this along in case you can help her with it. But I feel bad sharing this with you. It really should come from her." Again Jaden stared at Shane.

"If you feel that strongly about it, then don't share her secret with me. But, … if you think I could help in any way, then I do kinda need to know what could be upsetting her."

"Okay." Jaden nodded, convincing himself it was okay to share this with Shane, knowing he wouldn't be broadcasting this sensitive information to anybody. Jaden trusted Shane. "Okay. Her fiancé told her before she walked down the aisle that he had been having an affair with her maid of honor."

Shane winced. "Ouch."

"It was more than six months ago, but coming here was one of the changes she made for herself."

"With good reason," he said. "Well, I offered to be there for her if she needed something." Shane frowned. "I'll see if she comes back later today, and maybe I can get her to talk to me this time."

"Well, maybe let her tell you what went on in her past, before you tell her that you know. She might feel more like opening up to you that way."

"Sure, I can do that," Shane said, patting Jaden on his good arm. "You're a good friend to her."

"Okay, good enough," Jaden said. He wheeled toward his psychologist appointment, but inside he'd taken a boot to the gut. Shane had offered to be there for Brianna? Was something going on between the two of them? Jaden didn't even want to think about that. His heart wrenched a little just at the thought. And yet why wouldn't she be interested in Shane?

Shane was the opposite of Jaden. *I'm not fit. I'm a mess*

actually, and she is doing so much better for herself after her failed wedding.

Brianna deserved to have somebody. And Shane was a hell of a guy. No reason for her not to spend time with him. But that also meant that she wasn't interested in spending time with Jaden, at least not in that way. And he didn't think he could handle that right now. He sat outside the psychologist's office door, not even sure he was equipped to go in there.

Just as he was about to turn around and leave, she stepped toward him and said, "Definitely time for you to come in now."

He just glared at her.

She smiled. "The best time to get things out in the open is when you're angry and upset about something."

"But I would not be clearheaded at that time," he said reluctantly, as he wheeled into her room. "I don't really want to talk about it. It's just happened, and I don't know what to make of it."

"Interesting," she said in that smooth tongue of hers. He just glared at her. *Again.* She smiled and said, "Do you want some water?"

He shrugged and accepted a glass from her. And then he sighed. "I sound like a two-year-old, don't I?"

"I was thinking of an eight-year-old right now," she said, "but obviously somebody said something to upset you."

"Why would you think that?"

She chuckled. "It's what I do. Remember?"

He settled back into a sullen glare again, and her smile widened. He put down the glass of water and said, "This isn't working. I'm going back to my room."

"No," she said firmly. "This is our hour. If you don't

want to talk, you don't have to talk. You can just sit there."
She walked around to the side of her desk, opened a couple
files, and appeared to get back to doing some paperwork.

He stared at her in astonishment. "What's the point of
me sitting here if we're not going to talk?"

Immediately she closed the folder, faced him with an
expectant look, and said, "Perfect. What would you like to
talk about?"

And he realized he'd left himself wide open for that.
"The fact that I'm not whole," he said. "That I'm not as
good as a man who is whole," he snapped. "That up against
the normal males in this world, I'll come off in a much worse
way. What chance do I have of having another relationship?"
The words tumbled out without even giving him a chance to
make them coherent.

But she obviously understood. She settled back and said,
"Ah."

His glare turned more ferocious. "What does that
mean?" he snapped.

"It's a stage that every man here goes through," she said.
"It doesn't matter whether you're missing a finger or whether
you've got scars or whether you have internal wounds. That
question always comes up. *I'm not as good as others, so why
would somebody choose me over what is perceived as a perfectly
healthy and strong and fit male.*"

"Of course," he said. "It's part of human nature to compare ourselves to others."

"And how sad is that?" she said with a sigh. "Because,
yes, you're right. We do. But that doesn't mean that it's
something that we should do or that we want to keep
doing."

"Well, it's not like you can stop it," he grumbled.

"I wish we could," she said with a laugh. "But, no, you're right. So, what you have to understand is that all those *perfect people* you're comparing yourself to," she said, with a gentle smile, "are *not* perfect."

"Well, they sure look perfect to me."

"Of course because you're looking from a very jaded and one-sided point of view," she said.

"So what should I do instead? I'm supposed to sit here and think of all the good things that I have in order to compete with the others?"

"You'll never *compete*," she said, "because *competition* is the wrong avenue to even consider much less take. What you have to remember is that, inside, you *are* good enough. And that whatever woman you're looking to impress will be impressed *if* she's the right one for you." He snorted at that, and her smile deepened. "I presume we're talking about Brianna."

He froze. His gaze widened as he stared at her.

She nodded. "I thought as much."

"And how did you know?"

"Places like this," she said, "it's pretty hard to keep things like that a secret."

"Well, there isn't anything to keep *secret*," he said, "because nothing is between us."

"Are you not friends?" And one of her eyebrows raised delicately.

He could feel his insides clenching. But the honesty required of him at that moment had him speaking the truth. "Yes, we're friends."

"Good," she said. "I understand that Brianna could use a friend right now."

And, with those simple words, Jaden realized how he'd

made this all about himself. Without even thinking about what it was that Brianna wanted or needed. He took a slow deep breath. "That was a low blow."

"In what way?"

"Stop asking me questions," he said in frustration.

She placed her pen down, then leaned back, interlaced her fingers, and rested them in her lap. "Why don't you tell me what the relationship is between you and Brianna."

"She's a nurse. I'm a patient."

"So, it's professional?

"No. Yes." He frowned. "It's professional in that we're both here at Hathaway House," he said slowly, "but we're also friends."

"Good. Like I said, I think she could use a friend right now."

And again he struggled with that. He reached up, rubbed his face, and said, "Jesus, I'm a mess."

"So let's figure it out," she said.

He shook his head. "There's not a whole lot to figure out. I just suddenly realized that there was no reason for her to even want to spend time with me when perfectly healthy individuals are around who are well respected and are 100 percent physically normal."

"Like Shane?"

He glared at her, adding a groan this time. "You don't have a problem going for the jugular, do you?"

The corner of her mouth twitched.

He nodded. "Okay, so maybe Shane said something that set this off." He continued to glare at her. "How do you know?"

"I did see you in the hallway with him."

"Perfect," he muttered but then shut up.

"So? Shane works with a ton of people," she said. "He works with a ton of patients and many professional people. As far as I know, he's never had a relationship with anybody in this place."

"There's always a first," Jaden muttered.

"There are, indeed, firsts everywhere we look," she said smoothly. "But I do know that he's a good friend to all of us here. If he thought that somebody needed help or that somebody should reach out a hand, Shane would be one of the first ones to do so. He has done so many times already. It hasn't ever worked out to being a relationship for him though."

"That doesn't mean this won't happen now."

"No, probably it doesn't mean that, but neither does it mean it automatically will either. What you're listening to is the fear inside you. That part of you that says, *You'll never be as good as Shane, so why would anybody look at you?* You're comparing yourself again, and that's a downhill pathway that you don't want to go on."

"Too late," he snapped. "I hit the gas pedal in that direction at least twenty minutes ago. I haven't been able to stop yet."

"So, what is it you think that Brianna needs?" she asked.

"She needs a man who's dependable and who won't betray her," he said instantly. "Somebody who will be there for her when she's down and out. Somebody who she *knows* she can trust, even when her best friends are around."

"And why on earth," the psychologist said with emphasis, "would you think that Shane has any more of that than you do?"

He stared at her, frowned, and said, "Maybe he won't have any more of all that than me, but, given we're the same inside, everybody looks to the next level, and Shane definitely will win there."

"What makes you think she'll go to *the next level?* You've just said everything she needs, which fall inside a man, those things that make up his character, not his height or weight or the color of his hair."

"But there's more to a relationship than just showing up and being a good person," he complained. He saw that she was trying to keep a smile off her face. And he realized just how this all started to sound.

"Yes, there's *a lot more* to a relationship," she said. "There has to be that *click*, that connection that says that something special is between you. In my opinion, that comes first, whether it's as subtle as a Texas fall or as blunt as a lightning strike. You may not even recognize it at first. I doubt you can have that spark with two different people at the same time. Not if you're being honest with yourself. Not if you recognize the difference between lust and love.

"So, … even if she were to have that *spark* or some connection with two men, then, yes, maybe she would go down to the second layer. But she would do it on an instinctive level. She would measure the worth of one man to the other. It's not a conscious decision based on physicality. Like, *Oh, Shane is six-six. I prefer him over you, who's six-three.* It's not anything like that. Not for the women I know and call friends.

"First and foremost is the *click*. Then, the next level, the second level as you put it, is all those qualities that she needs. The trust that you spoke of. That honesty and communication. She doesn't necessarily need a man who can stand on his own two legs all the time. She needs a man who can stand on his two legs *figuratively*," she murmured.

Jaden sat here and groaned. "*That* is something I do," he said, staring out at the window. "I've always been a good provider and caretaker. I know how to get the job done, and I've always shown up to get it done. But things are different now."

"Only because it's a different job that you have now," she said. "Right now, your present job is healing. Your job is to show up and to get this done. Is there any reason to think that you have cheated anybody in that process?"

"No," he said. "I've done the best I could in that aspect."

"Exactly," she said. "So, remember. First is the *click*, and next is all those intangible elements that make a relationship work. It's never just about the physical fitness or the physical look or that the body pieces have to all be there. We're talking about you and Brianna, not some immature selfish person or a gold digger or a society wife in the making. We are dealing with you and Brianna here. So this is about something a whole lot more than your looks. And," she said, pointing her finger at him, "for all your provider instincts and your caretaker attitude, don't forget that Brianna makes her living as a caretaker too."

"Right," Jaden said, bowing his head. "In other words, I'm being foolish."

"Not necessarily," she said quietly. "Just acknowledge your feelings, as whatever they are, but don't get stuck on labeling them something when it could be something else. In other words, you need to talk to Brianna about this. It obviously upset you, and you two need to work it out." She waited for a response from Jaden but didn't get one. "Right?" she said louder, breaking through his melancholy for at least a moment.

"Right." After her silence, he looked up. "Right."

"And don't ever, *ever* knock your feelings in that way just because you might be acting foolish. You still have to honor the fact that that's how you feel."

"Just feels like everything is sideways," he muttered. "The minute Shane said he was reaching out a hand to help her, it just hit me that, you know? If he was reaching out, why would she look at my hand that's already out there?"

"But you're missing one vital part," the doctor said. "And that's the fact that she's already reached back for your hand."

He nodded and let out a heavy sigh. "No, you're right," he said. "She already has. … I'm just not sure she realizes it yet though."

Chapter 8

B RIANNA TOOK SEVERAL days off, just shoving her real issue into the back of her mind and moving on with the job of living before she allowed herself to pull out that one thought and look at it closer. Stuffing it away gave her a little bit of distance to detach from it and to see if it was true or not. She'd often seen scenarios in high school where some girls who were less than pretty hooked up with guys who were less than pretty because they accepted that they couldn't do any better. That the more attractive males were just above their grade.

And she wondered if she'd done that here as well. And that was such an insult to Jaden. She just couldn't even believe that the thought would have crossed her mind. But, at the same time, a little part of her—still so hurt and so desperate not to go through what she'd gone through once already—was looking for a much better relationship, when she hadn't expected herself to be looking at all. Not now. Not so soon. Obviously she still had issues. She wasn't ready.

Brianna quickly went through her morning routine, skipped lunch, and picked up yogurt and a bowl of fruit salad from Dennis after the noon rush was over, and headed outside. She knew she was avoiding everyone, but she just wanted to commune with nature and the horses.

This was her second lunch in a row out this way, and

Dennis raised an eyebrow but didn't say a word. She was even more isolated than normal, and that was probably not a good thing. As she sat out in the deep grass, she realized she'd tucked up against the fence, hidden from view. Lovely had come up within the fence and had laid down at her side. Appie was here too. Amazing how these beautiful animals knew she needed their peaceful acceptance right now.

Just on the other side of the fence, she could reach out and touch the llama. It was a perfect way to spend some time with them. Content to just be around them, she sat here and ate her lunch, while she wondered about how she'd made that slip from being a bright and carefully loving person to somebody who felt so hurt, so guarded, that she would even think along this line, this horrid discovery that had sent her into these last few days of deep soul-searching. And then she had to forcibly look at why she was attracted to Jaden.

And none of the reasons had to do with his physical body. Not that she wasn't attracted to him, to the whole person that he was. She had been most appreciative of his soul, his ethics that he lived by, his kind and respectful manner with her. His honesty when they spoke. She just loved spending time with him. His natural smile, his guts at how he handled his condition; with that contemplated, she sighed and then relaxed a little more as a load of guilt and condemnation slipped off her back.

It had been so hard to think she might have been that person. She was sure a lot of people might not blame her for it, but she blamed herself. Jaden deserved so much better than that.

Then one silent revelation ran through her mind. *You're a caregiver. You have a soft and kind heart. Be soft and kind with yourself too, as you are with others. Especially Jaden.*

She sat back against the fence post. She had been fully invested in all her patients; her attachments ran deep. Before, of course, she was in hospital or hospice wards with the terminally ill and dying, so not like now. Not like Hathaway House. Not like Jaden. So her caring deeply for this man wasn't about his disability. It was about his strengths. It was about her hope for something more to develop here. A future.

Which she couldn't and didn't have with any of her patients before. They were different.

Jaden was different.

She shook her head and stared at the Appaloosa. "Appie, it'd be so much easier to be a horse."

He just shook his mane at her.

She smiled. She looked over at Lovely and said, "You two are the odd couple, but you make it work."

There really wasn't any other answer for her but to move forward slowly and carefully. Not because of herself but because of Jaden. The man had come here to improve himself, to get as fit and as physically capable as he could. He wasn't down and out. He wasn't depressed. He was the one picking up his life and making the best of what he'd been dealt.

Yet here she was, moaning and groaning because some guy who didn't love her had left her at the altar. Big freaking deal. Sure, it hurt at the time, but she had also figured out how Gerald was not the right guy for her. Never was actually. She definitely needed to drop her mantle of self-pity and move on. She'd done that to a certain extent, but she had far more to do.

She'd had her time to feel sorry for herself over these past seven months or so, but that time of mourning the loss of Gerald had come and gone. Now, along with this, she also had to be kind to herself—something she forgot so very fast. When she'd gone home early that afternoon a couple days ago, she'd gone to bed and cried and bawled and screamed and kicked and raged at herself and at the world. But afterward, she'd felt immensely better. And she had laid there on her own, sorting herself out.

When she couldn't get very clear on the issue though—about her feelings for Jaden—she had shoved it all down inside her and left it alone. Only now, a few days later, could she actually take out all this baggage and unpack it all and take a closer look at what was going on. She had thought briefly about seeing one of the psychologists, but she wasn't even sure if that was an option.

It probably should be a mental-health option for everybody who worked here because working with all these people and seeing all their problems—and their successes—had put her own life in perspective and had made her feel bad for ever complaining about her petty problems. She had both legs, both arms, both feet, both hands. She had a solid back. She'd never been blown up or tossed around or shot or burned or stabbed or run over or any of the other myriad incredible injuries she'd seen here, both to animals and to humans.

And yet here she was, again today, having a boo-hoo because her life hadn't gone the way she'd planned it to. She should have known before the wedding that Gerald and she were not well suited for a lifetime, but she'd been blind. She'd seen the signs and symptoms of his affair. But Brianna had been so stuck inside her fairy tale that she hadn't stopped and taken a good look at what was truly going on.

Even her supposed best friend, Jenna, who was to serve

as her maid of honor, had been distant and backing out of everything that they had planned to do together. Again Brianna should have known. Sure, Gerald and Jenna shouldn't have done what they'd done, but Brianna should have also questioned them well before the wedding. Even though all her wedding-related bills were finally paid off, and she was technically free and clear of that event, she still couldn't write off the memories and the hurts.

Well, it was past time that she got rid of those. And it was also time to stop judging everybody else by the same token that only Gerald and Jenna deserved.

Her ex had been a jerk. There was no reason for him to do what he'd done—other than total selfishness and immaturity. Why couldn't he just break up with her first, before dating Jenna? But it was over now. Brianna's relationship with Gerald was long gone, and maybe Gerald and Jenna were happy now, together or not.

Wasn't it time for Brianna to find some happiness too?

JADEN WASN'T EXACTLY sure where she was or why he hadn't seen Brianna in a couple days. But, of course, every time he saw Shane, he appeared to be superhappy, whistling and cheerful. And Jaden immediately connected Brianna with Shane, as though that's why she wasn't around Jaden at all. He didn't know how much longer he could go on until he got an answer. He had talked himself into speaking with her just as many times as he had talked himself out of bothering to bring it up.

And yet, every damn time he did, it seemed so foolish to ask her if she was seeing Shane. After all, Jaden had no claim on her, and he and she didn't have anything other than a friendship. It didn't matter what his heart said. It didn't matter what he wanted. He hadn't made any moves toward doing anything about dating Brianna, and, if Shane had, and she had chosen that pathway, then all the more power to Shane. That's what happened when Jaden waited and just accepted the leftovers of what the world dished out to him. Because, if he wasn't ready to pick up and run with what he'd been offered, he was a fool, and he should be the one who ended up suffering for it.

Trouble was, he didn't even want to think along those lines. He didn't want to consider why he hadn't spoken to Brianna about this, *his feelings*—he almost laughed at that— or why he hadn't already asked her out on a real date, but neither did he want to see Brianna with Shane. That would completely change Jaden's whole attitude about being here at Hathaway House, and he admitted to himself that he might want to transfer out of here too.

He groaned for the tenth time.

"What's wrong with you today?" Shane asked.

Jaden had one big medicine ball in his arms, catching his breath, but Shane was panting too. They'd been working, lifting, carrying, forcing Jaden to use both his legs to build muscle in each. "Girl trouble," he said, glaring at Shane.

"Brianna again?"

Jaden shot him a look. "Maybe, but not likely."

Shane took his head at that. "You're not making any sense."

"It's not making any sense to me either," he said. "I just haven't seen her for a couple days."

"Yeah, she's been hiding again," Shane said.

"Why?"

"I don't know," Shane said in surprise. "You're the one who's got the insight into her."

At that, Jaden frowned. "I thought it was you."

Shane stopped, looked at him, and asked, "What?"

"I thought you had a thing for her?"

"You thought *I* had a thing for her?" Shane repeated slowly. "Why?"

"If the playing field becomes awfully crowded, I'm not putting myself into that competition."

Shane dropped the medicine ball hard. It made a *thunk* and reverberated against the wooden floor. "I don't *have a thing for her,*" he said with a clear and crisp voice. "But I work with her and I care about her, like I do everybody else."

Jaden studied him through half-lidded eyes. "So, you aren't interested in her?"

Shane lifted an eyebrow and then shook his head slowly. "No more than a friend. I thought you two had a thing?"

"If we have *a thing,*" he said, "why haven't I seen her? She's hiding from me."

"Or she's *just hiding,*" Shane corrected. "Don't you just love how, when anything goes wrong, we always think it's us to blame?"

"Well, that's because we usually *are* to blame," Jaden said, his heart lighter at Shane's words.

"Maybe, but I think, more often than not, it's because we aren't sure what's going on. So, we instinctively think we've done something wrong."

"Maybe," he said. "It's not an easy thing, understanding a woman."

"No, but, if you don't open up and try to communicate with her, it'll just get worse."

"I have *to see her* in order to communicate," he muttered.

He picked up the medicine ball and threw it with more force than necessary.

Shane *oof*ed as it hit him in the chest. "Maybe you should do that again," he challenged, and he threw it back just as forcefully at Jaden.

They went hard and fast, throwing a very heavy medicine ball. Jaden didn't even know what the weight of the thing was. But, every time it hit him in the chest, it was all he could do to brace for it. "So, is this actually helping me?" he asked after a few moments of several more hard throws as he gasped for air.

"Did it take some of that stress out of you? If so, *yes*," Shane said, glaring at him.

Jaden took several deep breaths, releasing each one. He remembered what Shane had said about the formation of his ribs and his collarbone and head, and, when he did the next toss, he could feel all kinds of things unlocking in his back and his neck, and he smiled. "You know what? I think it did help."

At that, Shane burst out laughing. "Good," he said. "Then it's all worthwhile."

"Are you sure? I could still use a massage."

"Yeah, but that's just because you're wanting a massage. It's not because you necessarily need one."

The two men grinned at each other.

Feeling much better, Jaden was glad that he had at least brought it up with Shane. Jaden still might not have any resolution, and he certainly didn't have any answers, but he did feel better about discussing things with Brianna. Now, if only he could find her, then discover the best way to talk to her, and see what had her so upset.

Chapter 9

L UCKILY BRIANNA ONLY had to ask off for that one
Friday afternoon, since she had the weekend free and
could take those days without bringing even more attention
to herself. So Brianna carried on sorting herself out through
the rest of the weekend, and then, on Monday, she felt a
whole lot better and had resumed her work schedule. She
still had some of this stuff to work completely through, but
one of the things that she had done for herself was she'd sent
an email to her ex. She told him that she'd forgiven him for
what he'd done, and she was sorry that their communication
was so poor that they hadn't discussed it well before the
wedding day, and she wished him well in his life. When she
sent it, she'd taken a deep breath and stepped back. And then
she immediately told Susan, one of her girlfriends back in
Houston, what she'd done.

Instead of emailing her back, Susan called her. "Did you
really do that?"

"Yes," she said. "I felt like I needed to."

Just silence was on the other end of the phone for a long
moment. Then Susan said, "You're a bigger person than I
am."

"It was holding me back," Brianna said quietly. "He
probably won't even answer me."

"Or you'll find out he's married to Jenna, and she's

pregnant, and everything you'd planned for is no longer coming your way."

"I didn't do it to get the cheater back. Obviously my plans weren't coming my way anyway, not with him," she said. "He went off with my maid of honor. My supposed friend."

"Well, I'm still here," Susan said humorously.

"Right, and I didn't mean it that way," Brianna said, shaking her head. "I just seem to be saying everything wrong right now."

"And I didn't intend to upset you about it," Susan said. "I know what you've gone through. And Jenna wasn't just your friend. She was my friend too."

"Right. The things that we do in order to hide everything we're going through," Brianna said. "I'm still angry at her. And I think I'm angry because I'm hurt that she would have done such a thing."

"Of course you're angry. Not only did you waste a lot of money on a wedding that didn't happen, but her affair ruined your relationship and what should have been your special day."

"And yet now that there's been the passage of this much time, I miss her," she said. "How wrong is that?"

Susan sighed. "You're not the only one," she said, "but we can't ever go back to what was."

"I know. I can't trust her, so I don't really want to resume any friendship with her again," she said sadly. After she talked to Susan some more, she hung up.

When she went to put her phone down, it buzzed. She checked to find an email—from her ex. Gerald had responded with, *You're a better person than I am.* She paused, thinking that was big of him to open his response this way.

She read the rest of his email.

*I wouldn't have forgiven me for what I did. I had no
business hurting you. I never intended to. But my relationship with Jenna was founded on a lie because I was
engaged to you. And neither are we still together. Like
you, I've done a lot of soul-searching. I don't really like
what I've seen. I hope you have a better future.*

Gerald

She sat back and stared out the window. "Wow," she
whispered, "I didn't expect that."

She frowned, set her phone off to the side, and wondered if she should respond. They'd been friends for a lot of
years. However, it was better to let sleeping dogs lie because
she didn't want to deal with him further or to resume that
friendship either. She just wanted some closure, wanted to
get that off her chest.

If they'd been smart, they would have stayed friends.
Once you become lovers and move into a much more
intimate relationship, everything changes. And, at the heart,
they'd still been just friends. She'd loved him, but now she
wondered if she'd been *in love* with him or had she loved
him just as a very good, close friend. Those were questions
that she would no longer get answers for because everything
was different now.

And that was a good thing.

AT THE END of the day, Jaden could feel the knot twisting in
his back.

He texted Shane and said, "I know the massage request

was tossed out earlier, but I'm starting to knot up pretty bad."

"Be there in ten," Shane said. "On your bed just in boxers under the sheet again, please."

Jaden slowly headed to his room. He was feeling old, especially after the talk with the psychologist. He'd also had a physical from the medical doctor as well, and now he was just tired out. As he made his way to his bed, he stripped out of his clothes down to his boxers, climbed up onto the bed, and collapsed.

Shane poked his head around the door about the same time. "Good," Shane said. "You're ready."

"Maybe not," he said. "I'm feeling pretty old and worn out today."

"Some days are like that," Shane said. "And that's for us who are healthy and without any injuries to deal with too." He quickly pulled the sheet over Jaden's hips and put something on his hands.

Jaden could hear the bottle open and close and then set on the bedside table.

Soon afterward, Shane's very capable hands started working on his shoulder blades. "Where are you knotting?"

"Side of the ribs," he gasped, "and the center of my back."

"Close your eyes and just rest," he said. Very slowly but very surely, he worked the knots out of Jaden's back, easing up the tenseness. "Was it something this afternoon that set this off?"

"Yes," he said. "You and then the psychologist."

"Right. Same thing again. So maybe it's all good, as you need to talk with Brianna sooner rather than later."

"What can I say?" he said. "I'm an idiot. I'll just apologize firsthand and save myself a lot of effort."

"And that won't do any good," Shane said. "A lot more is required. You need to discuss this with her. You need to hear her words setting things straight."

"And this is where I get to act like a two-year-old and say, *I don't wanna*," he said, mimicking Shane's tone at the end.

Shane kept working in silence.

Jaden was tired and worn out, as well as restless from all the uneasy thoughts and suspicions he had been battling for days, wondering just what he was supposed to do about any and all of this, if anything. Jaden let his eyes drift closed. By the time Shane worked all the way down to his thighs to his lower calves, Jaden was relaxed and at peace. "You're dynamite," he said. "If nothing else, I've certainly learned the value of a good hard massage."

"Well, this one wasn't hard. This was specifically for easing your tension and stress and loosening those knots," Shane said quietly. "But maybe, if you're lucky, you'll sleep now."

"It's dinnertime," he said. "I should get food, but I did eat a huge lunch."

"If you're not hungry, don't eat," Shane said. "If you want something light, somebody can get it for you."

"Maybe you're right," he said. "Maybe I'll just lie here and relax."

Shane finished up, then grabbed his jar and said, "Take it easy. If the knots come back again, let me know." And he walked out of the room, closing the door quietly behind him.

Jaden lay on his bed with his arms at his side, still in the same position Shane had left him, as Jaden again let his eyes drift closed. His mind was consumed with images from when he was a child and happy and carefree, a time in his life when he had nothing else to worry about except putting a smile on his face and having his every need—just the basics—covered. Food, a hug to know he was loved. And he had been absolutely happy. But just that memory reminded him of how different his world was right now. He no longer had family. He did have a couple friends, and Iain was one of them.

He opened his eyes, wondering if he should call him. Would he understand the need to touch base with someone? What Jaden really wanted to do was talk to Brianna. Just to have coffee outside and to know that he wasn't alone. And because of that, he didn't do it. He didn't even know how to open up a dialogue with her now. It wasn't that he had a problem, not with her, not since Shane had said he wasn't interested in her that way.

Jaden just didn't know how to bridge the gap that had yawned wide between them. He didn't know if he had created it or if she had, but it existed nonetheless. He still hadn't seen her in days, and it bugged him. He reached for his phone, brought up her number because she was part of his team, and sent her a quick text saying hi.

When he got her hello response back immediately, he smiled.

Then she immediately texted again and asked, **You okay?**

At that, he put down the phone and frowned because, of course, she was responding in her capacity as a nurse. The caregiver in her had risen to the forefront, and she was worried about him. And he didn't know how to reconcile that with the friend who he wanted her to be.

When another text came in, he stared in the direction of his phone, wondering if he wanted to check it. But he couldn't resist. He reached for it and read her message. **I won't make dinner. I was thinking about getting something a little later. I'm still pretty full.** He smiled. It seemed almost like a normal conversation for them. **Same here. Just had a heavy massage. Not going anywhere. Sounds like you need to rest. I'm fine.** But his response sounded stilted to his ears. Yeah, Shane was right. Jaden wouldn't get over his doldrums until he talked to Brianna. Something he really didn't want to do, yet he truly wanted to be on the other side of that conversation, back to normal with Brianna.

He sighed, tossed down his phone, and turned so he could stare out the window. His body was like fluid butter right now. He didn't want to move and didn't want to tense anything in order to make the muscles do much. It would be so much better to just ease into sleep.

But now his mind was awake, and he kept thinking about her and all the things that they had left unsaid. Then his phone rang. He was kinda happy it wasn't another text from Brianna until he could face her. He groaned as he reached for the phone, picked it up, and looked to see it was Dennis.

"Hey," he said. "Do you need some dinner?"

"No, I'm still full from lunch, and I'm not feeling very well. I'll just have a better breakfast."

"Coffee, tea, or something like warm milk?"

"No, I don't feel like anything," he said, "but thanks for offering."

After Dennis rang off, Jaden thought about how unusual

it was to have people be so concerned. But, as the sun slowly sank, he lay here in the semidarkness, not moving, his mind awash with thoughts and feelings and consumed with everything that had happened in his life and how different it was from the pathway he had hoped for.

When a tentative knock came at his door, he called out, "Come in." And he was startled to see Brianna. He stared at her for a long moment. "Are you okay?"

"I think that's my line," she said quietly, as she stepped in a little bit. She left the door open and said, "How are you feeling?"

"Odd, weird, disconnected," he said. "It's just … an off time for me right now."

"I can understand that," she said. "I feel the same." She shoved her hands in her jeans, her slim form moving quietly over to the window. "I like to look out the window at times like this. Something feels more natural about being out there than being in here."

"I get that," he said. "I was thinking about going outside and just sitting, but I didn't want to be around people."

He felt her start, and she looked at him and asked, "Do you want me to leave?"

At that, he didn't know what to say. He shrugged and said, "No, that's fine. I appreciate you coming to check on me."

"We're friends," she said quietly. "That's what friends do." She walked back to the door. "Have a good night. Maybe meet for breakfast?"

He thought about it, smiled, and said, "Sure, and thanks for coming."

And she stepped out, closing the door quietly behind her.

He felt as if he'd lost something special in that moment. Yet he hadn't so much lost anything as he hadn't reached out and connected with someone, and that could have been special. Maybe that was the problem. He'd had an opportunity, and he had missed it. Right then, just the two of them had been here in his room, and they could have talked.

Instead, he got caught up in his own weird mental state and didn't know how to even broach the subject of whatever it was that had pulled them apart. He sighed heavily, pulled the blanket over his shoulders, and let himself drift off to sleep.

Tomorrow. Maybe tomorrow things would be better.

Chapter 10

SOMETHING WAS OFF between them, and Brianna didn't know what. She figured the problem was hers since she had been the one who had made that horrible realization and had run. She had checked up on him last night, after she sat in her apartment, not being able to stop thinking about him. So she'd gone over to check, but he'd been different. Not exactly happy to see her, yet not maybe unhappy either.

She didn't know if something had gone on in his world or with his treatment to cause this. She was only privy to part of what went on with any one of the patients' days. She could read their charts, but, other than that, she wasn't there for everything that went on in their lives. But what she did see was usually amazing. Sometimes it was devastating, and sometimes it was good news accompanied by tears. If it was bad news, there were more tears.

She'd seen a lot of men cry in her lifetime. Being a nurse, she knew it was just part and parcel of being hurt. But here she'd seen more acceptance, growth, and determination that went way past the human norm. It's like every emotion was amplified in Hathaway House. She enjoyed it, but it was also wearing. It's like she was being bounced off the same emotional currents that everybody else was riding along.

Maybe those emotional currents were why she'd taken herself in such a crazy mental loop here the other day. Yet, with or without those currents, she also understood that the people here made this job so enjoyable. She felt like she was part of something which truly helped others, something that took them to the point where they could lead independent and useful lives again. Hathaway House gave them a jumping off point to the next phase of their lives.

As she got dressed this morning, she decided to thank Dani for taking her on full-time. Brianna hoped she had absolutely no need to worry about her job because this was one place where she saw herself staying for a long time. So much was going on here that Brianna felt part of something valuable, bigger than her, with job security as well.

Anytime a new patient arrived, she saw how Dennis immediately checked to see what they needed and what he could do to help. But not just Dennis. Everybody here was involved in some way along every step of the healing process. And Shane—although he was here, there, and everywhere—he ran a team of physiotherapists who always went above and beyond their duties. Dani set that good example by always being heavily involved in everybody's needs, whether a staff member or a patient or one of the animals here.

Hathaway House was a place of caring, and maybe Brianna didn't have any chance to *avoid* caring for these people, every single one of them. Maybe just being in this environment made her look at herself a little bit more carefully. The fact that she didn't like what she saw in herself gave her a chance to sit down and to reassess if what she thought she saw was actually what she'd really seen. Or was that fear talking, holding her back? Because, man, this place was full of fear too. Fear that the patient would never get better, fear that things would be even worse, fear that who they were inside wasn't enough.

The emotions just went on and on. Sometimes for the better. She was proud of herself for having contacted her ex, but now she didn't know what to do with the rest of that disaster. Should she contact her maid of honor too? Brianna was afraid of opening that door. They'd been friends since kindergarten. Maybe that was why it felt like a much bigger betrayal because of the length of time that she'd known Jenna. Was her friend hurting too? Should Brianna leave well enough alone?

She walked into the cafeteria, looking to see if Jaden was here. He was so busy, so happy, cheerful doing his healing thing. She had to admit she had changed here too in the short time since she had arrived. She hadn't really expected it. But did being around people who were healing automatically help her to heal? Did being around people who were striving to be so much better than what they were when they arrived mean that she was striving too? Was it like osmosis and just something that seeped into her soul? She didn't know, but there had to be a logical reason for this shift in herself. Maybe it was just a matter of timing.

"Good morning," said a woman behind her.

She turned to see Dani there. Brianna smiled and said, "Good morning."

"Are you looking for Jaden? Because I saw him in the hallway."

"Oh, good," Brianna said. "We were to meet and have breakfast together."

"Good," she said, as she stepped past her, but Brianna reached out a hand.

"I wanted to tell you," she said, "how much I really appreciate that you hired me full-time here. I hadn't realized how much of a change and an effect it was having on me, but I'm very glad to be here and to be part of something so special."

Dani looked at her in surprise, and then her smile and gaze warmed up. "You're more than welcome," she said. "Thank you for being a part of it. It takes people like you to make it special. It's not just about the patients. It's about how the staff and the medical teams act too and how everybody works together. It's also about what we do with ourselves while we're here, and I can tell you that we can do an awful lot."

"Isn't that the truth," she said. "I hadn't expected some of what I'm seeing."

Dani's eyes shifted. "Tell me more?"

Brianna shrugged. "I see people heal. I'm healing too."

Dani nodded. "And that is a phenomenon we have seen here before," she said gently. "It's hard not to when you see so many other people working and striving to open up their world. And, for that, I'm grateful for myself and for you." Then she moved ahead and got into line.

As Brianna turned around, she saw Jaden on his crutches. She looked at him and smiled. "Wow," she said. "I gather you had a good night's sleep."

"I did," he said, his smile bright and much more positive than she'd seen in a while.

He looked at her, then back at Dani and asked, "Problems?"

"No," she said. She waited for him to step into line beside her. "I was just thanking her for the opportunity to be here. It's nice to be a part of something like this."

"Agreed," he said seriously. "She's also a special person who has been through a lot."

"Right. I think Aaron is supposed to be coming back

soon, but I forgot to ask her."

"Maybe," he said. "I haven't met him myself."

"Neither have I," she said. "He's been at vet school the whole time."

"And that's a challenge in itself," Jaden said. "Long-distance romances are tough."

"All romances are tough," she said with a bright smile. She stepped into line and moved up with him.

"How are you feeling about yours nowadays?"

"Much better," she said cheerfully, realizing the truth in her words. "I contacted my ex and told him that I forgave him." At a strange sound coming from him, she turned to see Jaden staring at her in shock. She shrugged. "It seemed like the right thing to do."

"Not for most people," he said.

"No, maybe not, but it was holding me back," she said quietly. "I haven't contacted my girlfriend, the maid of honor, and I don't think I can do that."

"I couldn't either," he said, "but good for you for releasing your ex from that."

"He said he was surprised and that I was a much bigger person than him because he couldn't do the same thing if our positions were reversed. And he is no longer with my girlfriend. He said he felt like he cheated on both of us."

"He did," Jaden said. "Cheating never does anybody any good, and it only hurts all three of you."

"Well, he's free to move on. As for my girlfriend, well, she's made choices that she'll have to live with too."

Just then Dennis looked at her from behind the counter and asked, "What can I get you?"

"I'd really like an omelet," she said.

He moved off to the side, where the omelet station was,

and proceeded to make her a custom order. By the time it was done, her mouth watered. She looked at it on the plate, then back at Jaden, who was loading up on sausages and eggs and hash browns. She laughed. It felt good too because she hadn't laughed in a while. "This is a great place," she said. "Look at how different our choices were, and yet how excellent they both look."

"Exactly," he said. "We're blessed."

Dennis happily waved them on and served whoever was coming up behind them. Together, her carrying the heavily loaded tray, they moved outside into the early morning sunshine, instinctively choosing the same table where they had met. She smiled and said, "This feels like a reunion."

"It is, in a way. I haven't seen much of you in the last few days." He tried not to study her too intently. Last thing he wanted was for her to see how interested he was.

Her smile fell away. "No, you haven't," she said, "because I had some heavy thinking to do."

"With your ex?" He kept his tone brisk, as if he were curious but a little detached.

"No," she said. "My ex and I are definitely that. Exes," she said with a smile. "I've never been one to go backward in life."

"Good," he said with satisfaction.

"Oh, you like that, do you?" She cut into her omelet, a big smile on her face.

"Absolutely," he said. "I was thinking that we've become good friends while we're here."

"Absolutely," she said. Then she put down her knife and fork, as she continued to chew, staring at him. She leaned forward. "I haven't really made any friends here."

JADEN LOOKED AT Brianna in surprise, and she shrugged. "According to Dani and a few other people, I'm still putting out those stay-away vibes."

"I never listened to them anyway," he said, with a chuckle.

"Thank you for that." She sent him a huge beaming smile. "Because, if you had, we wouldn't be having breakfast together today."

"Good point," he said on a laugh. And he dug into his own plate. He inhaled the first part of his breakfast and finally slowed down enough to enjoy it.

"You were hungry," she noted.

"I was," he said. "I fell asleep last night, just after talking to you, and I slept right through the night. It was the best sleep I've had in a long time."

"And that's excellent news," she said. "You've come a long way."

He looked up at her over his forkful of food. "I feel like I have," he said cautiously. "But I'm still so far away from where Iain is that I know I don't dare get complacent."

"Whether you do or don't," she said, "it won't matter because you'll be the best that you can be, and that's all any of us can count on."

"I don't know that I like the sound of that," he said with a laugh. "I refuse to end up with less success than Iain."

She grinned. "Right. Keep that bar high. Now, if only we could live up to all those lofty ideals."

"Something about being here," he said, "makes me want to try harder."

"The people? The program? Or just the air?"

"Not sure," he said. "Maybe the whole package."

"Definitely magic is here," she said. "I'm affected too."

"Well, if you actually forgave your ex," he said, "that's a huge step forward."

"It is," she said with a smile. "I feel much freer. Like a weight's been taken off my shoulders."

"So, you dropped those walls a little bit," he said. "And, next thing you know, you'll be making friends."

"And see? The thing is, I didn't even think I was putting up walls," she said. "So how do I drop walls that I don't know I have up?"

"I don't know," he said. "But maybe just be consciously aware of it, and, before you know it, you'll have people being a little more friendly to you."

"And maybe I just need to be a little friendlier," she murmured.

"I think that's all part and parcel of the same thing. The wall stopped you from being friendly and stopped others from being friendly too. If you step forward and be a little bit more open to those around you," he said, "I'm sure you'll get the same feedback coming to you."

"Something to work on today," she said. "I'll see what happens."

"And you can check in with me tomorrow," he said, shaking his fork at her, "because everybody needs friends."

"Speaking of which," she asked, "when is Iain coming back?"

"Not for a few days yet," he said, settling deeper into his chair. "I still can't believe it. He's a completely different man."

"In a good way?"

"Absolutely," he said with a chuckle. "In the best way possible."

Chapter 11

B RIANNA HAD FULL intentions of reporting back to Jaden about how she was doing with dropping her walls and being friendly. But, at breakfast time the next day, she found herself even more withdrawn. As she sat here, nursing a cup of coffee, Dennis walked over and pulled out a chair, then sat down beside her. She rolled her head sideways, looked at him, and smiled. "How's Dennis's morning going?"

"Mine's fine," he said with that same bright and cheerful voice, "but you don't look so hot."

She chuckled. "Tired and a little worn out," she said. "I'm fine though."

He nodded ever-so-slowly and said, "Looks like your heart is heavy."

"What's this now?" she asked in a teasing voice. "Do you have X-ray eyes? Can you see my heart sagging in my chest?"

"Hey," he said, "I don't even need X-ray eyes to see that."

She smiled and tried to shrug it off, then gave up and said, "You know when you look at yourself, and you don't really like what you see?" After a moment of silence, she turned to look at him. But his deep penetrating gaze saw way more than she had expected. Flustered, she once again tried to brush it off. "I'm fine, honestly."

"A place like this," he said, "I think it attracts people who aren't fine."

She stared at him in shock. "You think Hathaway House is like a magnet?"

"I do believe that, at times, people need something in their lives, and it's different for every person. And, if they're open and willing to receive it, then it shows up." With that cryptic statement, he stood, removed her empty plate, and walked away.

He left her sitting here, stunned. Wouldn't it be nice to think that such a simple answer was why she was here? Yet she really didn't need to know why she was here. She was just grateful that she *was* here. But one of the unsettling thoughts that had occurred to her during the night was that her walls were there for a reason, sure, but it was not just because of her ex but more so because of her lifelong girlfriend, the cheating maid of honor.

This went back to Brianna still feeling so much anger about her girlfriend, even though she was working on forgiveness for her ex. And she felt she was pushing women away more than she was pushing men away. As if she expected men to be cheaters, and she would take them or leave them, depending on the propensity of each one.

But she was also expecting women to be liars and cheaters. As she wasn't moving toward a relationship with them, she was in danger of not ever having friendships again. She sat here, sorting her way through this conundrum. But it was just too convoluted, and she wasn't getting anywhere. Finally she stood, refilled her coffee, and walked back to her office. She worked steadily, avoiding everyone through the morning. Rather than going for lunch, she picked up a yogurt, a piece of fruit, and a bottle of milk, then headed outside to the pastures. There, she opened her phone and called her friend in Houston.

"What's up?" Susan asked.

"Am I different since the break up?" she asked bluntly.

"Yes," Susan said cautiously. "Everybody is. Including me."

"Oh." Brianna didn't know what to say to that. Because, of course, everybody in her circle would be affected to a certain degree.

"None of us can go through a scenario like that and not be affected," Susan said slowly. Her voice dropped a little bit. "Watching you go through what you went through was painful, and even I look at men differently now."

"I was supposed to drop my walls a little bit today," Brianna said by way of explanation. "Instead, just by observing what I was doing, I realized that my walls were thicker against women."

"Interesting," Susan murmured.

"And, of course, I probably caught you at a bad time, haven't I?" Brianna asked, wincing.

"No, not necessarily," she said. "I am at work though, so, if I hang up unexpectedly, you'll know that my boss has come in."

"I should have waited until you got home."

"Well, if it was so easy to wait, then you would have. But it obviously wasn't easy to wait."

"No," she said. "It's just one of the things that I was thinking of."

"And it's important to think on all of it, but don't hash it to the ground forever. At one point you have to walk away," she said. "Did you come up with anything major?"

"Just the fact that I'm blaming Jenna more than I'm

blaming Gerald."

Silence.

"How ridiculous is that?" Brianna cried out. "As if, in my mind, I half-expected Gerald to cheat, and that a part of me would be okay with it because that's what men did."

"For that," Susan said, "you need to look back at your parents."

"Do I have to?" she muttered.

"Your dad was a womanizer, and you grew up with that expectation. And, although you were horrified and terribly upset right before your wedding, I was afraid that you might have gone through with it."

"What does that say about me then?" Brianna asked. "Do I have such low self-esteem that I'm supposed to accept that behavior?"

"Obviously a part of you, the child inside you, believes that that's what men do because that's what you saw growing up. But the adult part of you struggles with that and wants something different."

"And what about the part of me that feels like Jenna was the bigger betrayal?"

"We've all been friends for a long time," Susan said. "The three of us, so I understand. I feel betrayed too."

"And how do I trust anyone now?" Brianna asked, the sadness sliding through her voice. "I'm trying to heal from this, but it's like I feel that I don't deserve more. At the same time, I don't want women friends because I know that their betrayals will devastate me."

"So, you're already putting out the expectation that another female friend will betray you?" Susan asked.

"I'm afraid so. Not you though," Brianna said hurriedly.

"Good," Susan said, "because that'll never happen. But,

like you, I've shut down a little bit too. I haven't made new friends, and I'm eyeing the friends who I currently have, wondering if they would do something so horrible to me as well."

"Right? Is it just something that we heal through time?"

"Maybe. Maybe we must understand that we can't foresee every incident in life, and we'll have to bounce back as much as we can. We also have to understand there isn't necessarily an answer to all these questions."

"I don't think I like that," she said.

Susan chuckled. "No, you always wanted answers. You always wanted clear-cut decisions that we don't have here."

"Is that so wrong?" she asked in a small voice.

"No, sweetie, it's not wrong. It's just that, right now, you're feeling alone. And you desperately want to make more connections and more friends, but, at the same time, you're petrified."

"Of course I am," she said, staring across the grass. "I would rather just stay with the animals."

"And yet that's not living," Susan said. "You've been hurt. You've been knocked down, but you did pick yourself up. You can't expect that same cheating behavior from other people because that's not fair to them. I bet Gerald and Jenna were one in a thousand. At least I would hope so," she said in a wry tone. "Most of the people around you would never do something like that. And they'd be horrified and offended to think that you viewed them in that same light."

"Which, of course, I'm not viewing them in that light," she said. "But, at the same time, it's not so much about viewing them as being worried that they might become that way."

"I think you just have to get back on that horse and ride

it again."

"And that's why people become loners and isolated in their houses because they'd tried it again and again and keep getting hurt."

"So, the idea here is, you learn from this and move on," she said. "And hopefully you'll make better decisions as to who your friends are."

"Jenna and I and you were friends for decades," Brianna muttered. "I thought I knew Jenna inside and out."

"I did too," Susan said. "And now I haven't had any contact with her since that horrible day."

"No, me neither," Brianna said. "I did check, but her Facebook profile is gone too."

"I checked all the social media sites and found no sign of her," Susan said. "I also checked in case she had married Gerald and was using his last name, despite the rumors otherwise."

"According to Gerald's recent email, they didn't get that far."

"Good," Susan said with a note of asperity. "It's not fair that they should be happy after all the chaos they've caused."

"I know," she said. "Look. I'll let you get back to work. I'm sitting here, trying to find the courage to face women and worrying they are all two-faced liars like Jenna."

"I think you just have to put your best foot forward and realize that, even if somebody else does betray you that way, you were better off knowing ahead of time and not going down whatever path they're stopping you from."

"So, take Gerald and Jenna as a gift and a chance to have a redo on that part of my life?"

"Absolutely," Susan said warmly. "And you gotta re-member that, while Jenna is living her own life and doing her own thing, she has to live with her own actions. The three of us were together forever. I'm sure she's got to be missing us too."

After they hung up, Brianna sat on the long grass, eating her lunch quietly. When a voice very close behind her called out, she turned to see Stan walking toward her. She stood near the fence and looked at him. "Hey," she said. "I hope you don't mind. I just came down here for some solace."

"It's the perfect place to be alone," Stan said. He was carrying two little kittens.

Immediately she put down the spoon and the yogurt in her hand and reached out for them. He passed them to her, and she looked at him, then smiled and said, "Who are these guys and how come you have them?"

"Their mother abandoned them," he said, "so we've been nursing them for the last couple days, and now hopefully we'll transfer them over to solid food."

She hugged them close, listening to their tiny meows in her ear. "They're adorable." But, even as she held them, they curled up in her arms, and their tiny little engines kicked in. "And they're so very trusting," she said in wonder.

"Even though they've been kicked by life and lost the most important individual in their world," Stan said with a smile.

Her sharp glance studied his face, but he didn't appear to have any idea how relevant his words were. For a moment there, she was afraid he'd overheard her phone call. She dropped her head against the two little tabbies curled up next to her and whispered, "But how do you trust after a betrayal like that?"

"Because instinctively we want to trust," he said. "We're all looking for a tribe. We're all looking for our people.

Sometimes we make mistakes, and we pick the wrong ones. In these guys' case, their mother abandoned them. But they'll transfer their affections to the next warm body and hope for a better life. And, if it doesn't work out, they'll get bumped, and they'll try again. It's in the nature of who we are to keep trying."

She nodded slowly. "And I guess, if they get hurt or bumped or injured along the way, it's just part of life, isn't it?"

"It's not only part of life. It's a very necessary step in life," he said. "If you never hit any hardship, you wouldn't grow." He reached out with his hands, and she gently placed the kittens in them. He tucked them up in his arms and said, "I'll take them back and let them sleep with their other two siblings." He gave her a gentle smile. "Enjoy your few moments. And I'm sorry. I didn't mean to interrupt you."

"No," she said. "That's fine. I needed that." As he walked toward the vet clinic, she realized how much she did need his words and the feel of those cuddly kittens in her arms. Because he reminded her of something else that she'd forgotten. If she never had hardships or trials in life, she would never grow. One stayed stagnant and supposedly happy in their ignorance, just coasting along. But, if no hiccups and no speed bumps occurred in life, one never really had a chance to learn how to handle them or to have an opportunity to climb up and over them.

It left their problem-solving abilities behind because people never had any problems to solve. She'd had a wonderful opportunity to learn to grow and to mend her heart and to move on and to not blame everybody else around her for it. And to not look at who would be a friend and who wouldn't be a friend, but being open to see what would come toward her. Because the world was full of strangers, and they really were just friends she had yet to meet.

With that realization, she could feel another huge weight falling off her shoulders. With a happy sigh, she collected her leftovers and garbage from lunch and headed back to the cafeteria, to the land of the living, where she really belonged.

"ON BOTH LEGS," Shane said.

Jaden complied, standing upright and balanced—as much as he could. "I notice I'm still putting more weight on my good leg," he muttered.

Shane nodded. "That's normal, but I want you to balance out your weight. I want you to put it as equally on both as you can."

Slowly, almost as if not giving himself a chance to trust that leg, he rested more and more weight on it. Then he slowly opened his arms and closed his eyes, feeling his body sway at the unnatural movement. "Well, it feels a little better," he offered tentatively.

"It should be *a lot* better," Shane said. "Understandably, you're not sure you can trust it because it has given out on you before."

"Well, it wasn't anything I could count on," he said with half a smile as he stared down at his big feet. "It's still looking pretty rough."

"That's an appearance thing," Shane said. "I want you to move slowly four steps toward me."

Jaden tossed his head slightly and took one step with his bad leg, then his good leg, then his bad leg, and then his good leg. "Feels like I'm hobbling," he said with half a laugh.

But inside he was thrilled. "Yet I am holding my weight."

"Now, turn around and go back," Shane instructed.

Turning around was a little more awkward. "The ankle is stiff," he muttered. "It's like walking on a two by four."

"And it will be for a while," he said, "because, although we're doing all these exercises and getting the mobility back, you haven't asked it to walk normally in a long time."

"And the surgeons and the pins all have had an impact," Jaden added.

"Exactly," Shane said. "So, it's a case of a lot of things having to pull together now. But we need to get that leg moving more, so less wheelchair, more crutches, but a whole lot more without the crutches."

Jaden looked at Shane in shock. "When you say, *a whole lot more*, what does that mean?" he asked.

"It means, I want you to do *more*."

"And at what point in time is *too much more* too much?" Jaden asked.

"Well, I'd like to say that we can go by touch, but I don't think we can at this point." He walked to the side and grabbed the crutches, then said, "Get these under your arms."

And, with that, Jaden immediately felt more balanced and also felt a huge sense of relief. He immediately took his weight off the bad leg.

"Okay, now you did that instinctively," Shane said, noting Jaden's shuffle of his feet. "But was it painful? Does it hurt to stand on that bad leg?"

"It's weird. It's odd. It's *different*, but I'm not sure that *painful* is quite the right word," Jaden said in confusion.

"And, when you think about it," Shane said, "just having the crutch under your arm—as an expectation of being strong enough to support you—was holding you back."

"So, a lack of trust?"

"Absolutely. Lack of trust. We'll have to work on that with the crutches. I want you to walk one length of this room using that foot as much as you can but with the crutches for support, *in case*."

Jaden made an odd face and said, "Well, you're the boss here."

But now knowing that the leg could handle some movement, Jaden slowly moved across the room and felt complete surprise at just how capable his right leg was. He walked down and back again, and even he could see that he was using the leg a little bit more and more, and the crutches were almost there just as a safeguard. By the time he got to the other end though, he was tired. "So, is it the leg that's tired," he asked, "or is it me?"

"Both," Shane said, a big smile on his face. "This is a major mile marker for you," he said. "Now, what we don't want to do is overdo it, so every day we'll do this until it's not so strange and keeps getting easier to do."

"Okay," Jaden said agreeably. "How long until this right leg builds up so that I can do this without the crutches?"

"Well, let's hold off on the wheelchair for the next two days, letting you rely on the crutches mainly," he said. "Use the wheelchair if you absolutely have to. Otherwise, try to get along with the crutches. And that's enough for today as it is. We've got some paperwork to go over." They went over his measurements and his improvements as well as his weight, which he was really surprised to see was up seven pounds. He stared at that and said, "Is that due to Dennis's cooking?"

"It's also the added muscle," Shane said, showing him

the differences in the measurements. "You're doing really well."

"Does that mean I'm ready to leave soon?"

He studied the figures, seeing the differences in the right leg measurements, and looking at his leg and realizing it really was different. "You're improving, but, no, not yet," Shane said. "Maybe in about six or eight weeks. It depends if this continues."

Jaden stared up at Shane in shock. "Will it continue?"

"Absolutely," he said. "Just because you can put weight on your leg doesn't mean that you're fully capable of crouching and bending and doing all that life demands of that leg."

"Wow," he said. "Do you think it'll get there?" He hated the fact that he heard such a tentative tone to his voice, that little bit of worry that maybe he couldn't get what he needed, what he wanted.

"I think you have the capacity to get that leg fully functioning," Shane said. "I haven't seen anything that makes me think differently."

"Glad to hear that," he said. "As in, *really* glad to hear that." He smiled. "Do you have those photos?"

"I do," he said, and he downloaded them from his camera to the desktop.

When he brought them up, Jaden looked at them and frowned. "I see no change," he said, disappointment settling into his heart.

Shane laughed. "That's because this is the one we took last time," he said. "Look at the first one, and here's the one we just took."

And, when he looked at it, he gasped. "Wow," he said. He stared at the stark improvements in shock.

"That's why we do before and after photos," Shane said with a note of satisfaction. "You see your leg every day and aren't really noticing the bigger changes over the weeks. You really have to understand how far you've come, and the only way to do that is to see where you were and compare it weeks later."

"Well, I'm really glad to see this," he said. "It makes a massive difference."

"It absolutely does," Shane said gently. "Now I suggest some swimming to work that leg a little bit more."

"I'm all for that," he said. "A little bit of swimming goes a long way in my world. Not to mention it makes my soul smile."

"And that's important too. So, go get changed, and I'll meet you down there."

"I thought you said we were done for today."

"Nope, just done here, right now, and done with the walking. Now we'll take the weight off and go work on those joints."

It all made so much sense. It was quite amazing. And, with a happy and very full heart, Jaden headed back to his room to get changed.

Chapter 12

B RIANNA WASN'T TRYING to avoid Jaden, but neither was she working hard to search him out. She was still finding out who she was right now. It was too new, too different still to come up against somebody who would notice. And yet, she could feel looks from a lot of various people as she walked around during her day. Again, she skipped lunch and headed out to the animals, not because she wanted to be alone but because she wanted to experience how different her view of the world was right now.

Even Mother Nature looked and felt different. It was so hard to describe, but like she'd been given a new lease on life. Everything smiled at her, and it felt wonderful. This was all just such an unusual feeling, and she didn't quite know how to encapsulate it and verbalize it. But a lot of good things were happening inside.

As she walked back from her lunch, she headed straight to her office. When she got to Jaden at the end of the day, she knocked on his door, stepped inside, and said, "Hey."

He looked at her in surprise. "Hey, stranger," he said. "Are you okay?"

She chuckled, "Yeah. It's just that things have been a little different, so I wasn't too sure who and what I was there for a day or two. Then I had a couple really decent awakenings, and I'm wondering who I am now." She laughed. A bright smile was on her face, and she knew that he was affected by it too because his smile was natural and happy as it came back to her.

"I like the sound of that," he said, his smile still there.

She looked at him and motioned to his leg, then asked, "How are you doing?"

"I'm doing great," he said. "Had another progress report with Shane, and I'm really getting there, so I couldn't be more pleased."

"Awesome," she said. "Sometimes we just have to take some time in order to get to where we're going."

"And I think that's really important," he said, "but I've missed you."

Her heart melted slightly. "I missed you too," she said. "And thank you for giving me the space I needed."

He nodded slowly. "I'm not sure that I gave it to you as much as you took it though." And then he laughed. "And, yes, you are within your rights to do so."

Instantly she regretted her radio silence over those days. "It wasn't even that," she said. "I certainly didn't want you to feel like I had walked away. I didn't want to push my negativity onto you as I made these fairly uneasy discoveries."

"Got it," he said. "Not to worry."

She shrugged. "But I will worry," she said, "because that's partly who I am."

He looked at her and chuckled. "And I have to admit, that's a really nice thing about you," he said. "You come from the heart."

She smiled. "You up for dinner tonight?"

"You asking me on a date?" he said in a teasing voice.

She beamed. "And if I was?"

"Oh, I'd take you up on it in a heartbeat," he said,

chuckling. "So, the answer is, yes, absolutely on for dinner."

"Good," she said. She checked her watch. "I've still got paperwork to do until my shift ends. Then I need to get changed."

"How about we meet outside the cafeteria a little bit after five, maybe five-fifteen?" he asked. "And, if we don't want to eat right away, why don't we grab coffee, sit on the deck, and just spend some time together?"

She flashed him a bright, warm smile and said, "Thank you. I'd really like that."

HER TONE DEFINITELY held a lightness to it. Jaden wondered at that. Had it just been his imagination? He had had a jam-packed afternoon, and, by the time he finally rolled back to his room, he felt fairly unsettled himself. A doctor's appointment, lab tests, blood tests, and then, of course, the inevitable shrink visit. He didn't know why he had to keep going. To him, each visit was the same, just on repeat.

"How's the relationship with Brianna going?" the doctor had asked.

Jaden shrugged and said, "It's a great friendship, and it's helping to keep me centered."

"Interesting comment."

"No," he said, "don't analyze it. It just is."

She chuckled. "Glad to hear that," she said warmly. "And glad that Brianna is settling in on her own."

"Exactly," he said. "If nothing else, you really want to have her stay here because she's good for us all." The doctor nodded, but an odd look had been in her gaze. He shook his head. "Why? Don't you like her?"

She looked at him in surprise. "Absolutely I do. I just wondered how she was settling in and if she was enjoying her time here. Might have to stop and talk to her about it."

That bothered him because he was afraid he'd started something. "Just that I'd prefer you didn't after talking to me," he said. "I wouldn't want her to think we were talking about her."

"Of course not," the doctor said.

Even as he left her office and rolled his way to his room, he realized that he still felt a little uneasy. And then he saw Shane, standing outside his doorway, staring at Jaden in his wheelchair. "I was tired," he said instantly.

Shane nodded slowly, but it was obvious he didn't believe him.

"Fine," Jaden said. "I was rushing because I was late, and I figured this was easier."

"Don't make a habit of it," Shane warned.

"I won't," he said, and he wheeled into his room, deliberately closing the door behind him. Only then did he allow himself to relax. "Thank heavens for having a room to myself," he muttered. He rolled over to the bed and got out, then gently crawled up on the bed and stretched out onto his back. For a place where he was supposed to be alone, a lot of the time just so much went on in his life. He had to wonder if that had an effect on somebody's healing. Of course he was healing and doing just fine, and this was a marathon, not a sprint. He had to remember that.

He didn't know why he kept going back to the wheelchair, except that it was easy. And he still felt more uncomfortable on his leg than off. But he'd have to remember to take his crutches tonight because, if Shane saw him again in the chair, Shane would probably question what

Jaden was doing. Even he couldn't quite understand it himself. It was just part and parcel, that whole *everything in a state of flux* thing.

He browsed the internet for a while, wasting time, until he would meet up with Brianna. He changed into a clean shirt and shorts and grabbed his crutches. He opened the door and slowly made his way to the cafeteria. In the dining room, he saw her standing off to the side, talking to a few people. He didn't know those people, but she talked in a bright voice. Which was fascinating. So she really was working on taking down her walls. He nodded. *Good for her.*

Part of the problem with crutches was it was almost impossible to grab a coffee or a tray or anything while his hands were otherwise occupied. He really hated using the crutches at mealtimes, finding them much more of an obstacle than the wheelchair. As he frowned at the coffee service area, Dennis came up and said, "If looks could burn, you would have exploded all these coffeemakers immediately. What's wrong?"

"What's wrong," he said, "is the wheelchair is easier, but I came on my crutches."

"Ah, Shane has got you relegated more on the crutches now, has he? That's a positive sign."

"Maybe, but it's much harder to get what you need here."

"So, tell me what you want," Dennis said, always agreeable. "And I'll carry it for you."

"But you shouldn't have to," he snapped. Then he took a slow breath and said, "Sorry. You're not the reason I'm pissed."

"Nope, I'm not," Dennis said. "You're pissed at yourself because you expect more from yourself. Just be patient. Give it some time, and you'll get there."

Jaden groaned. "It seems like you've seen so many of us that it's like we all go through the same stages."

"Well, I think most of you do share a lot of the same stages but not always at the same time or in the same order or in the same way," he said. "It depends on your own healing and your own body. But there's no point in grumbling about it." He poured him a cup of coffee and asked, "Are you waiting for dinner or do you want a treat?"

"You had these monster cookies at some point in time," he said. "Do you have any more of those around?"

"I sure do," he said. "Here, grab this, and I'll get you one." He handed him the cup of coffee and then took off into the back. The trouble was, Jaden was awkwardly placed. He shuffled ever-so-slightly, keeping the coffee steady while using his crutches. And then he realized it just wasn't working well. But still, he managed to get out of the way and into a corner, waiting on Dennis or Brianna to find him. Just as Dennis came back, Brianna saw him and detached herself from the group and came toward him.

"May I help you with that?" she said with a heartfelt smile.

"I've got it," he said, his heart sinking in frustration.

She nodded and, without saying a word, went and poured herself a cup of coffee.

When Dennis came back, holding a monster cookie, she rejoined Jaden, checked out the cookie, then looked at Jaden, and asked, "Are you going to share that?"

"Nope," he said, but his surly attitude was gone, and he was happily teasing her. "You can ask Dennis for one of your own."

Dennis chuckled as he pulled out a second cookie.

She rolled her eyes and told him, "You can tell how much a guy likes somebody when he won't even share his cookie."

"Cookies are sacred," Jaden announced. "Now, how about I carry the cookies, and you carry the coffees?"

They quickly swapped out what they were carrying so he had the two big cookies, as they moved slowly out to the deck.

"It's good to see you on crutches," she said, once they both sat down and got settled.

"Maybe," he said, "but I feel much more awkward and like I can't maneuver anywhere near as easily as I think I should."

"You probably felt that way about the wheelchair originally too."

"The wheelchair is comfortable," he said.

"Too comfortable?"

He shot her a sideways glance.

"Often people see the wheelchair as an extension of their own physical space," she said. "And you take them out of that, and it feels like they've been separated from something important. And then they ask you to walk with two sticks and to use your hands and arms to do it, so you can't carry stuff. And it just adds to the whole uncomfortableness of the new thing."

"And yet I've used the crutches since I've been here," he said.

"But you have slid back to using the wheelchair more."

"Is it a slide back?"

"I can't answer that," she said. "That's for you to answer."

Chapter 13

BRIANNA DIDN'T WANT to sound like she was preaching, and sometimes it was hard to separate the nurse she was from the concerned friend she was as well. But she was also feeling too good about herself to not want everybody else to feel this good too. "Sorry," she said. "I know you didn't even ask for my opinion. I forget to turn off my day as a nurse when I'm still here in the same surroundings."

He shrugged. "Everybody has an opinion," he said, but his tone caught her sideways.

"True," she said. "You're right. Everybody has an opinion, and, especially in a place like this, everybody has an opinion about what to do and what you shouldn't do. I guess the really important thing is, you have to do what you need to do for you, for your own healing."

He nodded slowly and stared out beyond the deck.

She wasn't sure what had just happened, but he was obviously not in the same good mood that he'd been in earlier. "Sorry," she said. "I shouldn't have mentioned it at all."

He just shrugged, then picked up his coffee and had a sip.

"How has the rest of your day been?" she asked in an attempt to change the mood.

He shot her a sideways look. "It's never good when the last visit of the day is with the psychologist," he muttered.

She winced at that. "After dealing with a lot of my own issues lately," she said, "I can see how that wouldn't be terribly nice."

"No," he said. And then he seemed to shrug it off. He smiled at her and said, "But we go through what we go through, and hopefully we'll come out the other side whole."

"That's what we keep hoping for," she said with a smile.

"You appear to be settling in."

"I feel better," she said slowly, "as if everything slid off my back a bit."

"Which is huge," he said, studying her.

Cautiously she responded, "It is, but it's also a little un-nerving. I've been … *off* all week. It's just recently that I realized how much I've been allowing the break-up to affect how I view everybody. Mostly women."

At that, his eyebrows shot up. "*Women?*" he asked. "That's not what I expected."

She chuckled. "I know," she said. "Unfortunately, as I was raised by a father who had a cheating heart, it's a behavior I almost expected from my ex. So, although I was angry and upset, I gave him an easier pass on his behavior because it was *typical male behavior.*" She ended this with a twist in her face. "And, of course, that's not fair. But I held my maid of honor much more highly accountable because she was my best friend. Since kindergarten."

"Interesting take on that," he said, "because it's not ac-ceptable for a guy to be a cheater, and you shouldn't have given him a pass."

"Exactly," she said. "But I'm working on the forgiveness part. As I told you earlier, I opened up a dialogue with him, just to get that closure, that sense of letting it go, and I am feeling good about the whole thing. But then I was surprised to realize how I had judged my girlfriend that much harsher because I figured she should know what I was going through and because we'd been such close friends. And how I've been holding women at a distance ever since."

"The webs we weave," he said quietly.

"Exactly." The two of them sat here in the gentle outside air; the dead heat was gone, but it was still hot. "I have no idea what's for dinner," she murmured, her head back and her eyes closed. "But I hope the crowd comes and goes, leaving it a little more peaceful in there."

"Does that go along with making friends?" he asked, a note of teasing laughter in his voice.

"Don't care if it does or not," she said. "I'm also a loner. The friends I had were friends I made in school, and I kept them all these years. I haven't really worked to make any new friends, and I didn't need to. I was feeling quite fulfilled by the ones I had."

"And now?"

"And now, I guess, I have room for some new ones," she said, "but they'll be on my terms."

"Good," he said. "You're making progress then."

"That seems like all we do here," she muttered.

"I think the revelations have to come in our own timing, not that we get to choose the timing," he said. "And not everybody here is on such a talkative path."

"Lots of them don't like to talk about this stuff at all. Maybe that's where we're unique too."

"Maybe," he said. "Can't say I feel like talking about my problems right now."

"Sorry," she said. "You're making such phenomenal progress that I just hope you can see how far you have come."

"Well, it docs help to do those progress sessions with

Shane, like I had today," he said. "But then he tells me to use my crutches, but I'd rather use the wheelchair. Yet the crutches are a step forward, and the wheelchair is a step back, but somehow I keep falling back into what's easy."

"Interesting," she said.

"And that seems to be everybody's favorite word too," he snapped.

She nodded. "It is, isn't it? It's because we come from such different worlds and what you're going through is so different from what I'm going through, and yet they're both valid."

He looked at her strangely for a moment. "You think my concerns are valid?"

Her eyebrows shot up. "Of course they are," she said. "You have your issues, and they're yours, but they're just as important to you as the craziness of mine. Most people would look at me and say, *Get over it.* They don't sense the validity behind my emotional trauma. Sure, I'm making it a bigger trauma by always focusing on it, instead of getting past it. But you have to get to a certain point before you can get past it."

"Right," he said. "I think I'm scared."

She looked at him in surprise. "Of what?"

"Your comment about the wheelchair being an extension of me made a valid point," he said. "I can count on it. I can't really count on the crutches, or at least I don't want to count on the crutches."

"Okay …"

"What I really want is to count on my leg, but I can't yet."

"Can't or won't?"

He looked at her sideways.

She nodded. "Won't."

He groaned. "It's so stupid."

"No," she said. "It's not stupid at all. The fact that you can walk on your leg …"

"But it gives out," he said.

"Is that something Shane can work with?"

"Yes," he said slowly. "It hasn't happened in a while, but you certainly don't forget suddenly ending up on the ground in immense pain because your leg gave out."

"Hence the crutches," she said. "And the more you use the crutches, hopefully the more you'll use that leg, and the more it'll build up."

"Something like that," he said. "Honestly I'm so tired of it all."

"The healing?"

"No, the mental conversations. Even the verbal conversations. It's just … It never ends."

"You're right," she said, "so let's talk about something completely different."

He looked at her in surprise and asked, "Like what?"

"Favorite movie."

"*The Green Mile.*"

She stopped, froze, and said, "Oh."

He frowned. "Yours?"

"*Avengers*," she said with a grin.

He nodded. "Okay, so that was pretty good too. Favorite song?"

"'Happy' by Williams, Pharrell Williams," she said immediately.

His eyebrows shot up. "I'm not sure I've heard that one," he said.

She pulled out her phone and found the song on

YouTube.

As soon as she played it, he nodded. "I really like that beat."

"I love everything about it," she said. "Favorite food?"

"Cookies," he said, holding up the big cookie in his hand.

"Okay," she said. "That would be a favorite treat. So, how about favorite food?"

"Steak."

They went back and forth, finding out and learning a little bit more about each other all the time. Finally she turned to look behind him and said, "You know what? I think the cafeteria is half empty now."

He twisted slowly, mindful of his back and leg, and nodded. "You think we can make it?"

"Absolutely." She hopped to her feet, grabbed their empty cups, and said, "You didn't eat your cookie?"

"Saving it for dessert," he said, "but I feel like I need to hide it from Dennis now."

She had big pockets in her long sleeveless cotton overshirt, and she stuffed them both in. "Come on. Let's go get food."

As they made their way through the line, she pushed two trays so that he could come behind her on his crutches. When they had filled both trays, she said, "I'll take the one over and then come back."

"There's got to be a way to do this," he said. He lifted his tray with one hand and shook his head, as if considering whether he should try it.

She looked out at the deck and again at his tray and said, "Well, let me take mine and give you a chance to see if you can figure it out." And she turned as she deliberately walked away.

JADEN LOOKED AT the tray, then at damn crutches, and grabbed the second crutch so that both were under one arm. Now he could grab the tray in the center, where he carried the bulk of the weight of the plate and took a tentative step, using the crutch for support. And that worked not too badly. He took another one. He made slow progress, but he was using his good leg and supporting his bad leg with the crutches. Finally somebody came up and placed a hand on his shoulder, then took the crutches out from under his arm and said, "Now try it."

He looked over to see Shane standing there, holding both crutches.

Jaden frowned and slowly adjusted his hands on the tray, then warned, "I could fall and send this everywhere."

"You could," Shane said calmly. "In which case, we'll have a hell of a mess to clean up. But it won't be the first time."

Jaden nodded and slowly gained confidence as he walked toward the table where Brianna sat.

He watched her jaw drop, and she immediately stood up and said, "Wow."

When he got there, he felt a huge smile splitting his face. "Right?" he said.

She looked back at Shane, who was walking beside him but holding his crutches. "Is he allowed to walk like that?"

"If he can walk like that," Shane said, "he should be walking like that. The crutches are just that—they're a crutch. Sometimes you need that. But too often you depend on it because it's something that you can count on. But they aren't necessarily the best thing for you." He waited until

Jaden had placed his tray down, and then, moving carefully, he shuffled backward, teetering a little bit as his steps were unsteady.

But Shane didn't reach out to help him.

Jaden moved the chair back and then slowly sat down again. "Wow," he said. "I forgot what it was like to be independent."

"Do you want the crutches, or do you want me to take them back to your room?"

Jaden took a deep breath, then looked at the crutches and said, "Maybe just leave them here in case."

Shane nodded and stood them up at the side of the table. "Just in case," he said. "You can carry them just as easily as I can." With that, he disappeared.

Jaden looked across the table to see the glowing delight on Brianna's face. "You look happier than I am," he said in a teasing voice.

"The progress," she said, "is massive."

"Well, it feels pretty darn good. I'm not as comfortable with that leg yet though."

"Of course not," she said with a wave of her hand, completely dismissing the issue. "You'll get there though. Every day you'll get stronger. And the more you can walk on that leg, the better."

"Yeah, that was part of what happened today," he said. "Shane took away my wheelchair."

She stopped in the act of lifting her fork. "He took it away?"

"Well, I wouldn't have said anything earlier, but, when I got back to my room, I got changed and was heading down the hallway with the crutches. I heard something behind me, and I turned to see him pulling my wheelchair out of my room."

She chuckled. "I gather he figured you were done with it."

He winced. "Yeah. I figured so too."

"It should be a celebration," she said gently, "because this is major progress."

He nodded. "It is, and it should be. And really it is," he said. "It's just new."

"New is different. And new is uncertain, and new feels unsteady. But every day you'll make it better, steadier, more stable."

He nodded. "I need to walk every day now," he said, "to build up that confidence in my leg."

"With the crutches or without?"

"Both," he said. "With the crutches, walk a bit, lifting the crutches and then using the crutches. You know? That off-and-on type thing."

"So, why don't we work it into our lunch break?" she said. "Either inside or outside, although outside would be nicer."

"Outside would be good," he said. "It's one of the big advantages of being here, isn't it?"

"It absolutely is. And we can get a picnic too, if you want. We could take a walk down the road, find a place sit down, eat, and then you get to walk back again."

He stared at her. "That sounds lovely," he said. "Are you sure you've got the time?"

"I've got the time," she assured him. "Besides, tomorrow is Friday. After that, it's a weekend."

"Have you got plans?"

"I do," she said. "I'm going to see my girlfriend Susan in Houston."

"Are you driving or flying?"

"I'm driving this time. It's just three and a half hours each way. Not too back for a quick weekend trip."

"Good," he said. "Iain is coming out this weekend too."

She beamed. "See? We'll both have friends to visit this weekend."

"I'll miss you though," he said.

"I'm only gone for the weekend," she said. "I'll be back Sunday night."

"So, have dinner with me and Iain," he said. "He'd love to see you again."

"Maybe," she temporized. "I don't want to insinuate myself into your visit, just in case Iain isn't happy about it."

"He'll be happy," Jaden said. "Don't worry about that."

Chapter 14

F RIDAY'S LUNCH WAS a resounding success. They walked a good hundred yards out, with his leg showing no signs of weakening. Then, they sat, had a picnic, enjoyed their break, and, on the way back, he lifted the crutches, and he slowly walked. "Shane said to walk without a limp," Jaden said with a laugh. "That's easier said than done."

"That's because you then favor the other leg," she said. "And I'm sure he doesn't want you to do that."

"Exactly."

They parted on wonderful terms, and she got up early Saturday morning, excited for a quick road trip to Houston.

As soon as her friend saw her, Susan exclaimed, "I haven't seen a look like that on your face in a long time."

She shrugged and said, "Well, that may be because I've met somebody."

"The same somebody?"

"Yes," she said, and the two headed off for shopping and then lunch, and the whole time Brianna told Susan all about Jaden's progress at Hathaway House.

"So, he has both legs and both arms? It's just a matter of getting his back and his right side improved? That structural integrity you mentioned?" Susan asked.

"Yes," she said.

"He's lucky."

"He is, indeed," she said. She found, as the day went on, that she felt lighter and happier just by being around Susan again. When they stopped for coffee, Susan reached across the table, grabbed Brianna's hand, and said, "I have to tell you how you seem like your old self again."

"I feel much better," she said with a laugh. "Understanding so much of what I went through and letting it go has helped. Seeing you again has been another huge help."

"We're not *that* far apart, especially if you fly in some times, and then I can fly in to see you too, although by the time you drive to the airport, deal with security and lineups it might be faster to drive," Susan said with a laugh. "You know what? Maybe we can do a girls' weekend every month or so."

"Wouldn't that be nice?" she said. "I could invite you over to my place. You have got to taste the food there."

"But all your meals are covered," she said. "How does that work?"

"Yeah, but I can also buy a guest meal ticket and have you come join me," she said.

"Oh, well, that's an idea too," Susan said with a laugh.

"It might be a nice break for you. Come visit at the pool, spend some time drinking coffees—fancy coffees, if we want—have dinner in Hathaway House or out in Dallas, and a relaxing evening back at my place. A sleepover, like old times."

"You're on," she said. Then she stopped and said, "Unless you've got a date with Jaden."

"I might be spending some time with him," she said with a shrug. "You'd be welcome to come regardless. I can also arrange my dates with him for any day of the week."

"That'll be interesting, how you will handle the relationship once he's not there."

"There is talk of him staying in the Dallas area though," Brianna said with a flush on her cheeks. "And I think that would be wonderful."

"That would be lovely," Susan said, all smiles.

Brianna told her friend about Iain and what he was doing in town.

Susan smiled warmly. "Sounds to me like he and Jaden both are much better men than Gerald was."

"Yes," she said. "I just didn't see what I should have seen."

"What was that you should have seen?" Susan asked curiously.

"I was looking for a father replacement," she said simply. "And I got him. My dad was a cheating SOB. And so was Gerald." She laughed. "He did me a favor, and I didn't even have a chance to thank him for that part of it."

"And I wouldn't thank him either," Susan warned. "It's nice to see him humble and looking back at his own actions and wanting to change, but don't ever give him a vote of approval for what he did."

"True," she said, laughing. "Now it's just a case of taking it slow with Jaden and seeing where it can go."

"Is it that serious?"

"I don't know," she said, "but I hope so."

"Wow," Susan said. "He must be special."

"He is," she said. "He's very special."

Sunday they decided to order in and have some girl talk, watch a movie—a relaxing day after the hectic one of yesterday. Then Brianna would leave shortly after lunchtime.

By the time she got home that evening, she was still feeling mellow and happy. She changed into a skirt and a pretty top that she'd bought on her weekend trip and raced up the stairs. Once there, she found a group of men off to one side. When she saw no sign of Jaden, she headed to his room. She knocked on the door, and, when she heard, "Come in," she opened the door and stepped in. He was fully dressed but lying on the bed. "Hey, are you up to dinner?"

He looked at her in surprise and nodded. He slowly sat up and then slid to the floor. "Sure. Iain had to leave early."

"Are you not feeling well?"

"I'm fine," he said. He stood up, and she walked over to where his crutches were, and he stopped her. "I'm gonna try to do this without them."

She nodded slowly and said, "Okay. You can take them if you want, just in case, or I can carry them."

"No," he said. "Thinking of this as our first date, I didn't want to go as a disabled man."

She stopped and stepped right in front of him, then said, "Even if you're in a wheelchair, on crutches, or walking as you are, *disabled* is a mental state. You might have a disability, but you are *not* disabled. You're one of the strongest and most capable men I've ever met."

He looked at her in surprise.

She shrugged. "I've grown up a lot while I've been here. I've also realized how naive and stupid I was when I was engaged to be married. My fiancé, God bless his soul, did me a favor," she said quietly. "Prior to him breaking up and leaving me at the altar, I hadn't really had any hiccups in my life. I hadn't had any opportunities to grow or to be stronger."

"When I first arrived, while I was sitting at that table, and then I saw you," he said. "I already knew you were strong and capable."

"That's because you didn't see my walls," she said, laughing.

"You didn't see my wheelchair," he pointed out.

"No. Not at first. But ... Well, I will admit that, with this soul-searching of mine," she said, "I did wonder about one thing. I was sick when I thought I found you attractive simply because you were in a wheelchair. As if I wouldn't have to worry about you cheating on me in a relationship because of that. And I hated myself for even considering that. Please forgive me. And help me forgive myself." She stared at him, searching for forgiveness. He frowned but not in disappointment. He was concerned. His hand gently squeezed her shoulder in support. He may have been silent but he seemed to be encouraging her to get it all out.

"So I'm very happy to say that I realized my attraction to you right from the beginning, and why I'm still attracted to you, is because of *who* you are and *what* you've survived and all that you've surmounted in your life." She took a deep breath and let more painful truths about her come to the surface. "I didn't have any of those to deal with in my life before my breakup. And, even after the break-up, I wasn't surmounting those. I wasn't challenging myself to rise above it all.

"Neither did I go on a search to learn something. I was just shoving it all away, trying to hide it from myself. That's what the walls were all about." She sighed. "So, the walls had to come down, but, at the same time, I realized that you've achieved so much in your life already that," she continued, "if anybody in this room is disabled, it's me. I hadn't had your challenges to work through. I didn't have any hiccups to find a way to get over.

"But now that I can see how much different I am today

from the person I was back then, I realized how naive and innocent I was. It's not that I'm older and more mature, but at least I'm a little more aware of who and what I am and who and what I need in my life."

"Wow," he said. "I wasn't really expecting all that to be going on in your life. No wonder you had to go off by yourself, to dig through that. However, I did think that maybe the wheelchair and this body weren't good enough for anybody." He took several deep breaths. "It's one of the things that Shane and I fought about. That I didn't see myself as being as good as him. He quickly told me off for that and made me realize this body doesn't define who I am."

"No," she said, "but the body does show who you are in the sense of how far you've come and how hard you've worked to get where you are. You don't see these steps that you're taking as progress, but I see it as tremendous gains, as tremendous strength and determination. I see it as a trailblazing path toward your future."

She reached out and gently stroked his cheek, then said, "You have no idea what a joy it is to see you on your own two feet like this. Myself? I've been on my own two physical feet." She looked down. "But I haven't been on my own two emotional feet. I've been wallowing. And, for that, I'm very grateful for this last week of discovery. It's been uncomfortable, and it's been difficult to face in so many ways, but it really feels like I've arrived somewhere, and that this somewhere is a place that I needed to come to."

"I agree, simply because you are so happy now." He motioned at the door. "Do you think we can start walking to dinner?" he asked. "I'm not sure how long I can stand."

At that, she burst out laughing and retreated to the hallway, then held out her hand. "Come on," she said. "Let's walk in together."

He smiled, took a few steps, and stopped close the door. And mindful to walk balanced and to not lean, they held hands as they walked down the hallway. "If we walk in there like this," he said, "everybody is gonna know."

"Are you ashamed of me?" she asked.

He looked at her in surprise.

She shrugged. "I haven't been a very good person."

"In what way?" he asked in astonishment.

"Well, I probably wasn't a good girlfriend to my ex, and I've certainly hidden all this time while I've been here," she said, "but I am different now."

"I can see that," he said. "I've noticed that you're much happier and certainly much brighter."

"Good," she said, "because that's how I feel."

"And that's BS about you not being good enough," he said. "How could you possibly even think that? I'm the one not here completely."

"Yes, you are. Your soul is much fuller than mine is. Mine's a little on the weak side, but it's getting better," she said firmly.

He started to chuckle. "This is a weird conversation."

She grinned at him. "Hey, I can agree with that," she said, "but it doesn't change the essential meaning behind it all."

"No," he said. "You're definitely worthy of me. I'm the one who felt unworthy of you."

"That's because you're looking at your current physical level and comparing it to Shane, probably the most physically fit of us all," she said. "As your leg improves, which it is obviously doing, you're improving by leaps and bounds. But the other parts, your emotional, your spiritual, your soul level? They're all dynamite. I'm working on those now too."

He squeezed her fingers. "Don't be so hard on yourself," he said with a smile. "Anything along that line comes to us naturally. I've been through a little bit more than you have, but, as life throws us different curve balls that we have to triumph over, we all duck or catch, depending on our style. Honey, in absolutely no way can you say you're less than I am."

"Okay," she said. "I'll give in on that." She was pleased to hear that he wasn't seeing her as any less after her shameful admission earlier. "It's funny," she said, "because I know that I needed to go through this, and I know that I owe my ex thanks for getting me here, but I hadn't realized how discarded he made me feel, like I was second-class. Like I'm not good enough."

"More BS," he said cheerfully. Just shy of the doorway, he stopped and looked down at her and said, "You're beautiful inside and out. I'm sorry that you went through what you went through, but it's his loss." He grinned. "And my gain."

She smiled a gentle smile. "Are you interested?" she asked.

The two of them stood toe-to-toe and eye to eye as they stared at each other.

"I'm definitely interested," he said. "You?"

"Oh, yes," she whispered. "Absolutely. I can't say I've met anybody quite the same as you in all my life."

"Ditto," he said. "And it makes everything that I've been through up until now more worthwhile," he added in a whisper.

"Why are we whispering?" she asked.

"Because it's a special moment," he said. "A very special moment." And he tilted her chin up ever-so-slightly, leaned forward, and kissed her.

She could feel everything inside her melt in joy. She gently clasped her hands on either side of his head, and, when he finally lifted his head, she looked up at him and smiled. "You're right. It's very special."

"So," he said, "a pact. Shall we move forward together in life as one?"

"Is that possible?"

"Absolutely," he said. "We'll bounce off each other on this journey of ours. When one slides back, the other will help, moving us up, so that we're again at the same level. And we can both go forward, but we won't ever hold each other back."

She shook her head. "Do you think we can?"

He grinned. "Sure. I'm an optimist," he said. "I'll be happy to show you the way."

She chuckled, and, hand in hand, they walked into the cafeteria.

As they stepped inside, everybody else stood, staring at them. Even Dani was here, with her father. Like they were awaiting Brianna's and Jaden's next move before they applauded.

Immediately Brianna's cheeks flushed deep red. Under her breath, she whispered, "Oops. We've been found out."

"Nah," he said. "We shared our first kiss, in front of *a few* of our friends. But I think there's a great way to handle this." He nodded, his gaze locked on hers. "The only way as we go forward is with a commitment."

"Are you sure?"

He grabbed her fingers and gently kissed each one of

them. He whispered in a serious tone to match the expression on his face, "I am. How about you?"

The tears pooled at the corner of her eyes. She nodded slowly. "I've never felt this way before."

"Good," he said, "because this is us, from now on, going forward. This is for us being together always, and this is for all our tomorrows." And he kissed her ring finger. "We'll fill this empty spot in a few days, if you don't mind."

Tears overflowed as she whispered, "Yes."

He smiled, took her in his arms, and this time he kissed her for real.

All around them, cheers erupted.

When he finally broke their kiss, her face was burning hot. But she had a beaming smile on it. "You do like to make things public, don't you?" she muttered.

"No," he said, "but what I don't want is to have our relationship be some secret, like we are ashamed or doing something scandalous." He let go of Brianna with his right hand to lift it, calming the crowd, still holding Brianna's left hand, to speak to all those gathered here. "As you all can see, she did say yes."

At that, the place erupted in cheers once more.

She stared at him, her eyes wide. She shook her head as more tears came to her eyes. And just when she turned to head toward the food aisle, Dennis stood in front of them with a bottle of champagne and two flutes. "You'll need food to go with this," he said, "but this is cause for celebration."

She looked up at him and smiled. "Did you have that ready?"

"I'm starting to understand this place," Dennis said with a big grin. "But nobody, nobody is happier than me to see this go down."

"Well, in that case," she said, "I'd love a glass of champagne with my dinner."

"Come on. Let's get you a table first," Dennis said. "Tonight you get personal service." And he led the way through the cheering crowd as the two of them walked together, Jaden a little slowly and a little awkwardly as they made it to the table at the far side. But, like a true gentleman, he stood and helped to push in her chair while she sat, and then he sat close beside her.

Meanwhile, Dennis popped the cork and filled the champagne glasses, then promptly left the couple alone. At least more alone in a roomful of others.

Jaden leaned across the corner of the table and whispered, "You look great tonight."

She smiled and said, "You always look great."

He grinned as they lifted their flutes and tapped them gently together. "To us. For now and forever."

She smiled and whispered, "To us."

And her heart had never felt better.

This concludes Book 10 of Hathaway House: Jaden.

Read about Keith: Hathaway House, Book 11

Hathaway House: Keith (Book #11)

Welcome to Hathaway House. Rehab Center. Safe Haven. Second chance at life and love.

Keith came to Hathaway House at his sister's insistence. For he has already given up on regaining the future she keeps telling him that he can find here or, for that matter, any other future worth having. And, besides, don't they know he's too weak for the trip and for the treatment and for any of the plans the team has for him? Don't they know he's broken beyond repair, and nothing they can do will fix him?

But apparently they don't because no one listens to him. Not the doctors. Not his sister. And definitely not the tiny woman who keeps delivering his coffee at 5:00 a.m.

Ilse, head chef for Hathaway House, rarely ventures out of the kitchen she manages. It's easier to deal with the groceries and the staff than it is to see the pain and suffering of those she feeds. But something about Keith and his frailty calls to her. She can't help but go out of her way to ensure he has everything he needs. Even though she knows she cannot keep their relationship on a professional level, once started.

Even if not in her best interests to do so. Because, in this case, surely Keith's best interests matter, so much more than her own.

Find Book 11 here!

To find out more visit Dale Mayer's website.

http://smarturl.it/DMSKeith

Author's Note

Thank you for reading Jaden: Hathaway House, Book 10! If you enjoyed the book, please take a moment and leave a short review.

Dear reader,

I love to hear from readers, and you can contact me at my website: www.dalemayer.com or at my Facebook author page. To be informed of new releases and special offers, sign up for my newsletter or follow me on BookBub. And if you are interested in joining Dale Mayer's Reader Group, here is the Facebook sign up page.

https://smarturl.it/DaleMayerFBGroup

Cheers,
Dale Mayer

Get THREE Free Books Now!

Have you met the SEALS of Honor?

SEALs of Honor Books 1, 2, and 3. Follow the stories of brave, badass warriors who serve their country with honor and love their women to the limits of life and death.

Read Mason, Hawk, and Dane right now for FREE.

Go here and tell me where to send them!
http://smarturl.it/EthanBofB

About the Author

Dale Mayer is a USA Today bestselling author best known for her Psychic Visions and Family Blood Ties series. Her contemporary romances are raw and full of passion and emotion (Second Chances, SKIN), her thrillers will keep you guessing (By Death series), and her romantic comedies will keep you giggling (It's a Dog's Life and Charmin Marvin Romantic Comedy series).

She honors the stories that come to her – and some of them are crazy and break all the rules and cross multiple genres!

To go with her fiction, she also writes nonfiction in many different fields with books available on resume writing, companion gardening and the US mortgage system. She has recently published her Career Essentials Series. All her books are available in print and ebook format.

Connect with Dale Mayer Online

Dale's Website – www.dalemayer.com
Facebook Personal – https://smarturl.it/DaleMayer
Instagram – https://smarturl.it/DaleMayerInstagram
BookBub – https://smarturl.it/DaleMayerBookbub
Facebook Fan Page – https://smarturl.it/DaleMayerFBFanPage
Goodreads – https://smarturl.it/DaleMayerGoodreads

Also by Dale Mayer

Published Adult Books:

Hathaway House
Aaron, Book 1
Brock, Book 2
Cole, Book 3
Denton, Book 4
Elliot, Book 5
Finn, Book 6
Gregory, Book 7
Heath, Book 8
Iain, Book 9
Jaden, Book 10
Keith, Book 11

The K9 Files
Ethan, Book 1
Pierce, Book 2
Zane, Book 3
Blaze, Book 4
Lucas, Book 5
Parker, Book 6
Carter, Book 7
Weston, Book 8

Lovely Lethal Gardens
Arsenic in the Azaleas, Book 1

Bones in the Begonias, Book 2
Corpse in the Carnations, Book 3
Daggers in the Dahlias, Book 4
Evidence in the Echinacea, Book 5
Footprints in the Ferns, Book 6
Gun in the Gardenias, Book 7
Handcuffs in the Heather, Book 8
Ice Pick in the Ivy, Book 9

Psychic Vision Series
Tuesday's Child
Hide 'n Go Seek
Maddy's Floor
Garden of Sorrow
Knock Knock...
Rare Find
Eyes to the Soul
Now You See Her
Shattered
Into the Abyss
Seeds of Malice
Eye of the Falcon
Itsy-Bitsy Spider
Unmasked
Deep Beneath
From the Ashes
Stroke of Death
Psychic Visions Books 1–3
Psychic Visions Books 4–6
Psychic Visions Books 7–9

By Death Series
Touched by Death

Haunted by Death
Chilled by Death
By Death Books 1–3

Broken Protocols – Romantic Comedy Series
Cat's Meow
Cat's Pajamas
Cat's Cradle
Cat's Claus
Broken Protocols 1-4

Broken and... Mending
Skin
Scars
Scales (of Justice)
Broken but… Mending 1-3

Glory
Genesis
Tori
Celeste
Glory Trilogy

Biker Blues
Morgan: Biker Blues, Volume 1
Cash: Biker Blues, Volume 2

SEALs of Honor
Mason: SEALs of Honor, Book 1
Hawk: SEALs of Honor, Book 2
Dane: SEALs of Honor, Book 3
Swede: SEALs of Honor, Book 4
Shadow: SEALs of Honor, Book 5

Cooper: SEALs of Honor, Book 6
Markus: SEALs of Honor, Book 7
Evan: SEALs of Honor, Book 8
Mason's Wish: SEALs of Honor
Chase: SEALs of Honor, Book 9
Brett: SEALs of Honor, Book 10
Devlin: SEALs of Honor, Book 11
Easton: SEALs of Honor, Book 12
Ryder: SEALs of Honor, Book 13
Macklin: SEALs of Honor, Book 14
Corey: SEALs of Honor, Book 15
Warrick: SEALs of Honor, Book 16
Tanner: SEALs of Honor, Book 17
Jackson: SEALs of Honor, Book 18
Kanen: SEALs of Honor, Book 19
Nelson: SEALs of Honor, Book 20
Taylor: SEALs of Honor, Book 21
Colton: SEALs of Honor, Book 22
Troy: SEALs of Honor, Book 23
SEALs of Honor, Books 1–3
SEALs of Honor, Books 4–6
SEALs of Honor, Books 7–9
SEALs of Honor, Books 10–12
SEALs of Honor, Books 13–15
SEALs of Honor, Books 16–18

Heroes for Hire
Levi's Legend: Heroes for Hire, Book 1
Stone's Surrender: Heroes for Hire, Book 2
Merk's Mistake: Heroes for Hire, Book 3
Rhodes's Reward: Heroes for Hire, Book 4
Flynn's Firecracker: Heroes for Hire, Book 5

SEALs of Steel

SEALs of Steel, Books 1–4
SEALs of Steel, Books 5–8
SEALs of Steel, Books 1–8

The Mavericks
Kerrick, Book 1
Griffin, Book 2
Jax, Book 3
Beau, Book 4
Asher, Book 5
Ryker, Book 6
Miles, Book 7
Nico, Book 8
Keane, Book 9
Lennox, Book 10
Gavin, Book 11
Shane, Book 12

Bullard's Battle Series
Ryland's Reach, Book 1
Cain's Cross, Book 2
Eton's Escape, Book 3
Garret's Gambit, Book 4
Kano's Keep, Book 5
Fallon's Flaw, Book 6
Quinn's Quest, Book 7
Bullard's Beauty, Book 8

Collections
Dare to Be You…
Dare to Love
Dare to be Strong…
RomanceX3

Standalone Novellas
It's a Dog's Life
Riana's Revenge
Second Chances

Published Young Adult Books:

Family Blood Ties Series
Vampire in Denial
Vampire in Distress
Vampire in Design
Vampire in Deceit
Vampire in Defiance
Vampire in Conflict
Vampire in Chaos
Vampire in Crisis
Vampire in Control
Vampire in Charge
Family Blood Ties Set 1–3
Family Blood Ties Set 1–5
Family Blood Ties Set 4–6
Family Blood Ties Set 7–9
Sian's Solution, A Family Blood Ties Series Prequel
    Novelette

Design series
Dangerous Designs
Deadly Designs
Darkest Designs
Design Series Trilogy

Standalone
In Cassie's Corner

Gem Stone (a Gemma Stone Mystery)
Time Thieves

Published Non-Fiction Books:

Career Essentials
Career Essentials: The Résumé
Career Essentials: The Cover Letter
Career Essentials: The Interview
Career Essentials: 3 in 1

Printed in Great Britain
by Amazon

78149746R00108